The Man Comes Around

Around

The Wayfaring Strangers Book I

Alexander G. R. Gideon

For all those I've lost.
I hope Ukufa made you smile when he opened the door.

Contents

1. The End of Endings   1
   Part I

2. Versus Terminus   56
   Part II

3. Salvator 3:56   100
   Part III

4. What Lies Beyond   133
   Part IV

The End of Endings

Part I

That his father could move his arm at all was a miracle. A *wasted one*, Kholo thought, turning his eyes to the sky and hoping the goddess could hear his words. *If you're to grant him a miracle, give him his life instead.*

His father placed a hand on his cheek, and a moment later Kholo felt the man's strength fail. His hand started to slide from Kholo's face, and he placed his own over it, holding it still. His father's skin felt like old, brittle paper, and he wondered how the fire of fever in his flesh did not set it ablaze. The man cracked open an eye, flakes of dried mucus fleeing from its corners and tumbling down his ashen face. Kholo could only imagine how much pain he was in, but still the man smiled when he saw his son.

"I am sorry," he said, his voice barely audible over the echo of the crowd outside the alley where he laid.

"You have done me no wrong, father," Kholo replied, proud that the tears he held back hadn't slipped into his voice instead.

"I have. I have never regretted bringing one as beautiful as you into this world. But you deserve so much more than the life I have given you."

A series of coughs wracked his body, and Kholo stroked his hair until it subsided.

"I have never needed a high-rise apartment, or the screens and implants *they* use to convince themselves the world is what they wish it, rather than what it is." Kholo gestured toward the end of the alley and the people passing by with no concern for them, holoscreens gathered around their heads like storm clouds and flashing like lightning. "We have lived in such a way they think impossible. And I have been happy despite what they, or you, think. They call us homeless, but we are not."

He placed his hands on either side of his father's thin face and brought his own close. He could not hold back the tears any longer, and they fell upon the frail man. "*You* are my home, father. And I am yours."

His father smiled again, a single tear leaving a dark trail through the dust on his skin.

"Then I am sorry you are losing your home."

"Do not say that," Kholo said, his voice breaking. "I am going to save you. I almost have enough credits for your treatment."

"I am beyond that," his father said with the slightest shake of his head. "But you are not. Save yourself. Promise me you will live. Find another home. Do not die on these streets as your mother did. As I am destined to."

"Father—"

"Promise me,"

"I promise," Kholo said, unable to deny him, or the inevitable any longer.

"Good."

His eyes fluttered shut, and he went limp in Kholo's arms. Kholo's breath caught in his throat.

"Father?" he choked out, hot panic stabbing him in the kidneys and robbing him of his full voice. He placed a finger to check for the rhythmic beat of his father's heart. It was faint, but there. He still lingered. For now.

Kholo gathered him in his arms and leaned against the opposite wall of the alley. He should stay in his blankets Kholo knew, threadbare as they were. But if this was to be his end, Kholo pledged that he would not face it alone. His eyes burned as his tears fell unchecked and unchallenged. He laid bare all the love he had for his father, sobbing harder than he could ever remember in his life. There was no son in all the vast countries of Etgaelna prouder of their father than him. And he wept that no one would know when such a bright light ceased to shine.

In his sorrow, Kholo felt eyes on him. He looked toward the end of the alley, and found a man standing in the opening, his sharp eyes fixed on them. His skin was the impossible dark of a moonless night, his head bare of any hair. He was clad all in grays and whites, a stark contrast to the colorful styles of those on the street around him. His lack of holoscreens made him stand out more than anything, though. Kholo met his gaze and held it for several long moments, and even from this distance, he could see the eldritch depths in the man's eyes.

"Ukufa," Kholo whispered in reverence for He Who Holds Your Hand in Shadow, the guide to the promised tomorrow. He smiled as a group passed in front of him, blocking him from Kholo's view. When they passed, he had disappeared as if he had never been.

All through the afternoon and unto the setting of both the red and yellow suns, Kholo held his father. They did not have much in the way of food or drink, but what little remained Kholo offered to him. He would not regain consciousness enough to eat, and Kholo could only manage to get him to swallow a single mouthful of a nutrient supplement drink he had managed to steal. Darkness fell, and still he cradled his father to his chest.

"You are not alone," Kholo whispered to him.

At some point in the night, exhaustion took him, and he slept, his dreams fitful. In them, he wandered the streets, calling for his father. He became more frantic in his searching until he felt a hand on his shoulder. Kholo stopped and looked back to find Ukufa once more. The Man in Shadow looked at Kholo with a kindness he had never seen before.

"He is gone," Ukufa said, his voice so deep Kholo felt the vibration in his bones. "Not yet. Be at peace. You will find another home."

When he woke, the Red Sister, the first of the twin suns, had just declared her presence in the northern horizon, bathing the land in her bloody light. And as Ukufa said, his father was gone.

Kholo had no more tears to shed, so he lifted his father in his arms and carried him from the alley out onto the street. Curious eyes followed him until they caught sight of the brand above his right eye. They averted their gaze then. They were Banished after all. Unclean and unworthy of their consideration.

His father had fallen ill for the first time only a few years before. Kholo often tended him while his mother went to the city to try and get the things needed to treat him. It ended up being the death of her. Few dared to accept money from the Banished when they managed to have any at all. She was caught stealing, and the shop owner killed her. He received no punishment for it either. A Banished wasn't a person, after all.

Kholo could not leave his father alone while he tried to go to the city, so eventually he resigned himself to bringing him here to get what they needed. He had never been to the city before, but he heard stories from his parents of its wonders. Of how technology connected the world, improved life for the masses, and brought so much happiness.

But he had yet to see that happiness. Or the connection. So immersed were they in the screens around them, they did not look at each other. Many chose not to even talk, instead sending their thoughts in text form to each other, or to the stall keepers on the streets. Transports thundered by overhead by the thousands, all spewing exhaust and poisoning the air. He had not been able to get a real breath since he stepped foot here. His parents had once been a part of this world, and he knew they missed it terribly. But he had never known it, and now that he saw it, he did not want to.

The crowd of buildings and crush of bodies fell away when he stepped onto the grounds of the Temple of the Sisters. The twin spires of the cathedral towered over him, and he bowed his head. Banished were not permitted to look upon Their house. He laid his father at the doorstep and knocked three times, then seven, then five. The sacred acknowledgment of the

Sisters' trials. With one last look at his father's face, so peaceful in death, he turned his back to the temple to leave.

"How dare you," a voice said from behind.

Kholo turned and a woman in red robes slapped him across the face. Reeling back, he covered his stinging face with a hand.

"You are unclean and unwelcome," she said, spitting on his feet. She cast her eyes down onto his father before looking back up. Planting a foot in Kholo's chest, she kicked him down the stairs. A cry tore from his throat as he tumbled halfway down the flight.

"The enforcers come," the priestess said, scowling down at him from the top of the stair. "Honor the Sisters and atone your sins in death."

She turned and swept back into the temple, the massive doors slamming shut behind her with a resounding boom. The tramp of running feet reached Kholo's ears, and he saw a group of men and women in red and white battle gear charging across the temple grounds toward him.

"I am sorry," he said to his father, wishing he could see him. This far down though, he was out of sight. Sending up a prayer to the Sisters to accept him into their arms, Kholo turned and ran.

Shouts of protest rose all around him as he wove through the crowds. Entranced by their halos of screens, most did not notice him as he sped toward them, forcing him to shove them out of the way. He knocked dozens down in his haste to escape the enforcers that followed, grim faced and intent upon his death.

Kholo did not know where he could run to escape the fate that pursued him. No matter how he twisted and turned through the alleys, the enforcers would not be deterred. Panic beat a rapid tattoo in his chest, and he begged his legs to carry him faster. His father's voice echoed through his thoughts, driving him on.

"Promise me you will live. Do not die on these streets..."

Turning down a tiny alley, his breath caught at the sight of Ukufa at the other end. He smiled and turned, vanishing from sight to the left of the opening. Kholo squeezed down the passage, the rough concrete scraping against his skin on either side.

"Stop running and be free of your sins," a woman called from behind him. He heard the scrapping of her battle gear against the concrete and scrambled faster through the crevice.

When he finally squeezed out, he looked in the direction Ukufa went. The Man in Shadow stood at the end of the next alley as well. Again, he stepped out of view, and Kholo rushed after him. *He is guiding me*, Kholo realized. *Just as he guides the dead through the darkness to the Promised Tomorrow so the Shadow will not devour their spirits.*

The enforcers gradually lost ground while he followed Ukufa. For hours they threaded through the darkness of the city, and Kholo wondered if at the end he would find himself with his father again.

Then he turned a corner and Ukufa was nowhere to be seen. Kholo scoured the area for a trace of him but found none. No pounding footfalls met his ears, but he knew the enforcers would not abandon their search so easily.

A child stepped into sight from an opening a bit farther up the way. He waved at Kholo to follow and hurried back the way he had come. Kholo sped after him, unsure of where the boy wished to take him, but sure it was better than wandering aimlessly through the maze of alleys.

The child led him a short way to what looked like a pile of trash and detritus. The boy pulled a broken screen bigger than himself out of the way and squeezed in behind it. Kholo followed suit and found a door hidden behind it. The child smiled at him, and the door opened. A man with braids that reached his waist stood in the jam, a knife in his hand. He saw the child and relaxed, though he studied Kholo with caution.

"The enforcers were chasing him," the boy said. "Can we protect him?"

The braided man nodded, his face softening as the caution fled his eyes.

"Welcome brother," he said, stepping back to let them inside. He closed it behind, clicking a myriad of locks into place.

The boy led Kholo down a long tunnel-like corridor and out onto what looked like a stage. It seemed this had once been a theater of some kind. They had erected a dozen makeshift tents where there had once stood seating. A mix of fires and a few artificial lights brightened the space. The scent of cooking meats and roasting vegetables caressed Kholo's nose and set his stomach rumbling.

As if summoned by the sound, a woman with a shaved head and an angry scar that ran across her scalp and down her neck put a bowl of rice in his hands.

"Eat, you'll need your strength," she said with a smile.

"Thank you," Kholo croaked, realizing how long it had been since he had water. Another man, his own jagged scar running down the side of his dark face to split his beard, handed him a jug. He drank from it, wanting to down the entirety of its contents. Without knowing the extent of their provisions, he took only a few mouthfuls though. The man brought Kholo over to one of the tents and sat him in a ragged chair before a cook fire.

Though he tried to refrain, his stomach demanded he fill it as fast as possible. An older woman laughed while she watched him devour the rice as if he had never eaten before. The scarred woman took the bowl from him the moment he finished, replacing it with a skewer of meat and vegetables. Kholo tore into it with relish, making short work of it. The older woman offered him a pipe when he set the skewer down. He shook his head and she nodded.

"Thank you all for the help," he said loud enough to be heard by most in the theater, glad for the strength that had returned to his voice.

"You are most welcome," the man with the braids said, taking a seat next to him. "How did you come to have the enforcers hunting you?"

"My father died this morning," Kholo said, staring into the flames. "I took him to the Temple of the Sisters so he could be with them now that his banishment has ended. One of the priestesses saw me and called them."

"I am sorry for your loss," the braided man said, putting a hand on his shoulder. "What was his name?"

"Oshiro," Kholo said, smiling at the feel of the name on his lips. Rarely had he ever spoken it.

"We shall speak of Oshiro here so that his name is not forgotten," the braided man said, squeezing his shoulder. "I am Ahluma. And you?"

"Kholo."

"You are welcome here for as long as you need, Kholo."

Placing his own hand over Ahluma's, Kholo smiled up at the man. Rare had it been that he had felt comfort from anyone other than his own family. He looked around the fire and a dozen others gazed at him. The kindness in their eyes brought tears to Kholo's own.

"Thank you all. Life has been too difficult for too long, and I appreciate the moment to catch my breath," he said, wiping his eyes.

"We must protect each other," the woman with the shaved head said from across the fire. "Especially with the Temple's newest decree."

"I have not heard of a new decree," Kholo said. "My family lived in the outlands. Precious little news makes it out that far."

"Then do you know of the Sotiras?"

Kholo shook his head.

"Show him, Fain," Ahluma said. The shaved woman nodded and came to sit next to Kholo. A screen winked to life in front of her, catching Kholo by surprise. "The woman I got the neurolink from did not have use of it anymore."

Kholo wondered why that might be but held his tongue and focused on the screen in front of him. A woman in medical whites stood at a podium, a thousand recording devices aimed at her. Fain put her hand on the back of Kholo's head and the woman's words blossomed into his mind.

"—For all the people of Etgaelna, not just our nation," the woman said to the gathered. "Four decades ago, Neren Indalo changed everything that we know about existence when he proved that human will, when combined with Latent Universal Potential, can reshape reality. My team has expanded upon the discovery, and we have found a solution to the greatest problem we face as a species. Death."

The screen shifted to a man in black robes, his close-cropped red hair odd against his browned skin. He seemed to stare into Kholo's soul, making him uncomfortable.

"It has been three years since High Artificer Suhasini announced the completion of the Sotiras and began imbuing it with human will in an attempt to end death. The United Artificer's Guild remain skeptic to her claims, and many warn of the dangers of attempting a working of this magnitude. But people all over Etgaelna have flocked to the Emerald Sprawl to add their will to the Sotiras to cure the world of death."

The rest of the world fell away as Kholo stared at those words. Cure the world of death. High Artificer Indalo proved the effect human will could have on reality forty years ago, and there had always been high hopes for what the discovery meant. But death was a fact of life; an inevitability. Could it really be ended?

His father's voice echoed through his thoughts. "Promise me you will live. Do not die on these streets..."

If the working succeeded, he could do nothing *but* keep that promise.

"What has become known as the Great Working is nearing completion, with its casting set for the day after tomorrow. In two days' time we'll know if the only thing certain in life is no more."

The screen winked out, and Kholo looked at Fain, eyes wide.

"That broadcast went out yesterday, so the casting happens tomorrow as long as they can get the last bit of will needed," Fain said. "Each person can only give their will once though, and there are only so many willing to add theirs. There are rumors that they might not be able to get enough."

"This has lit a fire in the Temple of the Sisters, though," Ahluma said, his face grave. "Since the doctrine dictates that the Banished cannot be absolved of their sins until they die, they've sent their enforcers out in unprecedented numbers to put every Banished they can to death. They say they want to save our souls. But I know you've seen how they sneer at us. They just want us exterminated."

"No wonder they pursued me so hard," Kholo whispered, horrified. Ahluma nodded.

"It all ends tomorrow though," Fain said with a smirk. "Once the Great Working is complete, we will be untouchable."

"Only once we reach Simahla," Ahluma said with a shake of his head. "If we stay here after we become deathless, the Temple will simply round us up and imprison us until the end of existence. I would rather die than face eternity that way."

"Why Simahla?" Kholo asked.

"Because they've driven the Temple from their borders and declared themselves a safe haven for the Banished," Ahluma said.

"'Banishment ends at our borders,' their Council declared," Fain said, her voice so full of hope that it could not help but lift Kholo's own heart. "In the Emerald Sprawl, we will be free."

"You are welcome to come with us," Ahluma said, poking at the fire to stir the coals. "Our commune will stay in place here until after the Great Working is cast tomorrow, then we will make the journey once surviving the distance is guaranteed."

"Is it safe to stay here?" Kholo asked, gesturing around. "Can the enforcers not find us?"

Fain shook her head.

"It is highly unlikely. This theater has been abandoned for over a century. A relic of the past before these neurolinks made such places forgotten."

Kholo nodded, but her words had not driven the anxiety from his chest. A hand gripped his shoulder again, and he looked up at Ahluma standing over him. The big man gave him a gentle smile.

"I see how unkind life has been to you and how alone you feel," the big man said, giving him a gentle smile. "Come rest with me."

Kholo hesitated for only a moment before allowing himself to smile as well. He stood and let Ahluma lead him to one of the tents. The interior was bare with only a few bags and a pile of blankets that acted as a bed. Ahluma lowered himself onto the blankets, pulling Kholo after him. He held Kholo close, resting his head on his wide chest. All the tension left Kholo's body as they laid there, the steady beat of Ahluma's heart in his ear.

"You've been strong for far too long, friend," Ahluma whispered, stroking Kholo's hair. "So, for tonight, rest, and let *me* be strong in your stead. You are safe here. With me, and with us."

The tears began to stream down Kholo's face, and he wrapped his arms around the big man. All the grief he had not had time to face stuck him at once, and Ahluma continued to stroke his hair as he sobbed into his chest. Kholo let out everything; all the pain, fear, and sorrow he had held for so long.

Eventually he had nothing left to feel, and his tears dried. Never once did the rhythm of the man's heart change, and its steadiness finally lulled Kholo into slumber. Just before sleep took him, Ahluma whispered again.

"Rest well, friend. Tomorrow the world shall be a better place."

Kholo's parents came to him that night. His father, young and healthy as he was in Kholo's childhood, grinned at him. Oshiro patted his back, though he never said a word. He stepped back and Kholo saw his mother then, with her beautiful braids so like those of the man who held him while he slept. She hugged him, and Kholo held her tighter than he had ever held anything else in his life. He breathed in her scent. The scent of home and a happy family.

Kholo felt eyes on him, and he looked up to see Ukufa again. He stood at a distance, watching the trio, his expression unreadable. Kholo's mother moved back, holding her son at a distance and looking him over.

"You have become a fine man," she said with a smile.

"It is good to see you, mother," Kholo said, wiping his eyes. He looked past her to his father. "I am sorry I could not save you."

"You saved me more times than you can ever know," Oshiro said, shaking his head. Ukufa appeared next to him, placing a hand on his shoulder. Oshiro looked up at him, his smile growing sad.

"We have to go now, my son," his mother said, hugging Kholo again. "But we will always be watching."

She let Kholo go and moved back to stand next to his father. He reached out for her hand,

and together they gave their son one last smile before they faded into the ether. Ukufa remained, and he turned his eyes on Kholo then.

"Remember the words of High Artificer Indalo," he said, his voice as deep as the ocean. "All things are possible until proven otherwise."

Then he was gone.

The explosion jolted Kholo awake. Ahluma sprang upright with him, alert in an instant. Without a word, they ran from the tent into a nightmare. The back wall of the theater now had a gaping hole in it, and a dozen red and white clad Temple enforcers flooded through, strikers sparking in their hands. Screams rose all around as the other Banished scattered, desperate to escape.

"Run," Ahluma shouted at Kholo.

"But I can—"

"Run!" he shouted again, pushing Kholo toward the door he had entered from and away from the enforcers. Kholo grit his teeth, but did as the man said, sprinting toward the exit.

He passed like the wind through the small camp. Halfway through, Fain appeared at his side, keeping pace with him.

"Ahluma asked me to keep you safe," she said, her face hard as stone. Kholo did not argue. In only moments they vaulted up on the stage and raced behind it to the door. None of the other Banished had managed to gather themselves enough to get to the exit, and Fain fumbled with the locks to get the door open.

When the final lock clicked open, Fain wrenched the bolt back and threw the door wide open. They stumbled through and out into the small alley and Kholo looked to Fain for direction. She pointed down the alley to their left.

"That way," she said, taking off down the alley. Kholo followed close on her heels. They reached a junction and Fain stepped out into the intersection of alleyways a moment before Kholo.

A striker lashed out from one of the branches, catching Fain in the face.

She screamed, both from her shattered nose and from the striker's electrocution. Kholo slid to a stop as Fain collapsed. The enforcer stepped out of the branch path and drove her striker into Fain's belly. Her body twitched at the surge of electricity, but she made no sounds. Kholo knew she was already dead. The enforcer looked up at Kholo who realized immediately he should have already been running. He turned to do just that and ran into another enforcer.

Colliding with him felt like running headfirst into a boulder, and Kholo fell back. He had barely registered that he hit the ground before rough hands picked him up again like he weighed no more than a stuffed animal. The enforcer held Kholo aloft, his feet dangling off the ground. He brought his face close to Kholo's, a scowl cut into his face.

"Looks like a couple rats escaped the nest," he growled. His breath smelled like he had just eaten a three day old carcass, and Kholo gagged.

"Sister's blood, you're touching it," the woman said from behind, her voice dripping derision.

"Please, just let me go," Kholo said quietly, doing his best not to antagonize them further.

"You need to be cleansed before the blasphemer traps you in your sins for eternity," the man said.

"Do not make me do this," Kholo said, reaching up and grabbing the enforcer's wrists.

"Do what?" the enforcer said with a scoff.

Kholo raised his knees, ramming them into the man's belly. Without any real momentum behind it, the strike was weak. But the enforcer had not expected it and it threw him off balance. His grip slipped, and Kholo broke his hold, dropping to the ground.

He rolled to the side, anticipating the other enforcer's rush, coming up on his feet facing her. She swung at him, and he dodged back, her striker crackling as it passed two fingers from his face. As his back met the wall, Kholo saw the other man had recovered and was only a step behind the woman as they both rushed him. Kholo pushed off, using the momentum to drive his foot into the woman's belly. She fell back into the path of the man's striker which he had aimed at Kholo's head. It connected with the woman's neck instead, and she convulsed as she screamed as the electricity shot through her. It took only moments for her to die.

The enforcer did not slow his rush, even with his comrade dead. Kholo stepped into the man, slamming a fist into his wrist, making him drop the striker before they collided. He folded over the enforcer's back and threw his arms around his neck. The enforcer twisted as he tried to slam Kholo into the ground, throwing him off balance. He rolled across Kholo who used the momentum to get the man under him and pin his legs with his own. Kholo wrapped his arms around the man's neck again, squeezing as hard as he could as he tried to get the right purchase. The enforcer scrabbled at Kholo's arms, but he ignored the man's flailing. Once he got the right grip, Kholo squeezed harder, focusing on keeping his hold as the enforcer fought to free himself. His flailing gradually weakened until at last he went limp. Still, Kholo continued to squeeze until he was sure the man was not just unconscious. Eventually, Kholo released his hold and pushed the dead man off. He lay on the ground, his breathing ragged.

He heard a muffled explosion, and he knew the enforcers were still attacking those in the theater. He could not linger here. He rolled and rose to his hands and knees. Looking up, he caught sight of Fain. He crawled toward her as a sob wracked his body. He could barely see through his tears when he reached her, and he pulled her up to his chest. He sat there with her, rocking her body back and forth while he wept.

It was all too much. She had died because of him. Because she tried to protect him. His mother and father were gone for the same reason. Why did everyone he cared for die? And he himself had taken two lives. Yes, they fully intended to kill him. But they were someone's children or sibling, or perhaps parent. Kholo had taken them from those that cared about them. That loved them. All he wanted was to escape death for his father, and instead he had dealt it.

Kholo did not know how long it took for his sobbing to subside, but he thanked the Sisters no other enforcers had found him. Wiping his eyes, he looked up and froze at the sight of Ukufa at the end of the alley. He watched Kholo with those dark eyes and Kholo couldn't read his expression. He blinked, and Ukufa was gone.

Wiping his eyes again, Kholo got to his feet. His mother had been military before her banishment, and she'd taught Kholo how to defend himself. Her knowledge saved him. Her knowledge let him continue on and fulfill his father's last wish. Right or wrong, it was done. All he could do now was keep going.

Kholo could not stay in Ingozi. The Temple was far too zealous in their campaign against the Banished. He needed to get to Simahla and the sanctuary the Emerald Sprawl offered. The only way he could hope to manage that would be to board a transport to the city. But even if he could reach the transport center his lack of holoscreens storming around his head would immediately raise suspicion. He looked over at Fain and her own words ran through his head.

"The woman I got the neurolink from did not have use of it anymore."

He knelt beside her and turned her on her side. The unit was small, curving around from the base of her skull to just behind her ear. It shone a smooth, shiny black, like a shard of obsidian. The unit slid from Fain's skin easily. It must have undocked automatically when Fain died. The squelching of its removal turned his stomach. The thin tendrils that connected to its user's brain stem writhed like spider legs and Kholo grimaced at the thought that they would soon be inside of his own flesh. Feeling around at the back of his head, he found the base of his skull. After taking a deep breath, he pressed the neurolink to his skin in the same position he had seen on Fain.

Within seconds a sharp pain made him gasp. The sensation of those tendrils wriggling their way inside of him was worse, and he grit his teeth as they groped around. The movement settled out and every muscle in his body went rigid. He had no way to describe the sensation that followed. The neurolink had started the process of fully incorporating itself into his mind and senses. The process took only a few minutes, but minutes felt like lifetimes with the feeling of something groping through his entire being.

At last it finished, and Kholo's muscles relaxed again. He realized he was on his hands and knees, staring at the ground while he tried to catch his breath. A screen appeared in front of him showing an image of the woman who represented the neurolink's AI.

"Good morning, Kholo," the woman said, her voice echoing in his head. "I will be your guide while using your neurolink. What would you like to call me?"

Kholo looked down at the woman who had tried to protect him.

"Fain," he whispered.

"Then I will answer to Fain from now on," the woman said. "How can I help you today?"

"Please guide me to the nearest Transit Center."

"I would be happy to activate destination assistance for you," The new Fain said. Another screen winked into being. It had a small map in the upper corner that showed an overview of Kholo's current position in Ingozi. In front of him, a small readout accompanied arrows that showed him where he needed to go.

"Thank you, Fain," he said, both to the AI and to the woman who had given her life for him.

Kholo looked around, tracking how the holo-screens moved with him. He once thought he might feel more like he belonged in the world if he had his own neurolink. But the screens in front of him now only felt incredibly unnatural.

With a glance at the map to ensure he headed in the right direction, he set off down the Alley. Just before he rounded the corner, he glanced back at Fain. Her head was turned toward him, and Kholo realized he had not closed her eyes and they seemed fixed on him.

"I'm sorry," he whispered as he left her behind.

Not even Ingozi's streets had prepared Kholo for the amount of people in the transit center. Thousands upon thousands, enough to make him feel unable to breathe. He ducked back into the access corridor he had come through, clutching his chest. The streets had not bothered him, and neither had the theater. But the thought of stepping out into that crush made his chest feel so tight, he thought his ribs might pierce his heart.

"Your heart rate has risen drastically," the new Fain said in his head. "From your last visual input, am I correct in guessing this is from the crowd in the transit center?"

"Yes," he said, panting. The neurolink's ability to monitor him left him feeling sick. It felt as if some parasite had infested him.

"Would you like me to assist in calming your body?" Fain said. The real answer was no. He did not want to rely on the link for anything. But he also knew he did not have time to figure out how to handle the crowds on his own.

"Yes," Kholo said through gritted teeth.

Within seconds his heart rate started to drop, and his breathing slowed. The panic faded enough for him to think, and he peeked back out at the station. The amount of people still looked overwhelming.

"I suggest looking at individuals in the crowd as you move through it. Focusing on single people can take your attention off the crowd as a whole," Fain said.

Though every fiber of his being told him not to, Kholo stepped out into the crowd. Panic tried to crawl back up his throat and he tried to follow Fain's advice, keeping his focus on the faces of those he passed. First a woman with almond eyes and pale skin, doing her best not to look at anyone as she hurried through. Next a man with much darker skin and long black hair, guiding a little boy that looked like a miniature replica of him by the hand. Then the oldest woman he had ever seen with loose skin the color of sand shuffling along holding on to the arm of who he imagined was her grandson.

Fain had been correct. Looking at everyone in the crowd as individual people helped with the over-stimulation. The map of the center made sure he went in the right direction. Kholo plodded on, glancing up from the faces around him to the map every once in a while, to keep his bearings. It worked, but the Sisters protect him, the center was huge. He walked for most of an hour, and still the red line stretched into eternity on the map.

The people around him constantly jostled into him. Generally, people gave the Banished a wide berth in an effort to keep from touching the spiritually unclean. But Kholo had covered his head in a wrap he had found along the way, positioning it low enough to cover the brand over his right eye. The Temple forbade hiding the brand, but Kholo found he did not much care to follow the decrees of a Temple that condoned genocide. No one refused to meet his eye, either. At first it only increased his anxiety, but they tended to smile when they did, and that simple kindness filled him with both joy and a deep sadness. He understood then that his parents had never cared about the technology of the world. This was the life they had wished for him.

At last, the bay came into view, along with a line of travelers waiting to pass through the gates to board the transport. New Fain had guided Kholo through the process of purchasing his ticket with the small number of credits he had loaded into the system. All he needed to do was bring up the appropriate screen to be scanned as he passed through. Simple. But life had never allowed itself to be easy for him. As he stood in the line and waited for his turn to pass through, wondering all the while when things would turn.

It did not take long.

Shouts sounded from somewhere farther down the center. Kholo turned with the others in the line to look, concern instead of interest painted on their faces. The gates opened then, and the line began to move forward. Kholo kept pace, though he continued to watch for what might have caused the sudden din. The shouting grew closer as Kholo approached the gate. He was next in line with the group of enforcers broke into view through the crowd.

"Your heart rate has risen drastically again," the new Fain said in his head. "Would you like calming assistance?"

"Not now," Kholo growled, stepping up to the gate. "Just bring up my ticket."

The screen winked into existence before him, and the scanner on the gate read it. The white doors slid open, and Kholo stepped through. He did not look back as he walked down the access hall to the transport itself. With every step he expected to hear the enforcers shout for him to stop. But the words never came.

A man in sleek blue robes greeted him at the door of the transport. He scanned Kholo's ticket again, then directed him to his seat. A woman was seated next to him, though she was already fast asleep with her head resting against the window. He settled in, thanked the attendant for his assistance. It did not take long for the other seats to fill, and within minutes the attendants moved to close the hatch. Just before they did, Kholo caught a glimpse of red and white.

"Get out of our way," the enforcer growled at the attendant from just outside of the hatch.

"The Temple's enforcers are not permitted on any transport bound for Simahla," the attendant said, his tone firm.

"We will not allow the Banished we seek to leave," the enforcer snarled, trying to push his way into the transport. The attendant placed a hand on his chest and pushed the man back out with surprising strength.

"The interior of this transport is under the same legality as Simahla," the attendant said, his voice full of disdain. "As such, the Temple and its enforcers have no power or jurisdiction here. Whoever this Banished is you seek; they are no longer banished here."

"Do not make us move you," the enforcer said, the ignition of a striker flashing in the hatchway. The attendant raised his hand and aimed his gun at the enforcer's face.

"You would fail."

Neither of them said anything for several moments, and Kholo gripped the arms of his seat.

"The hatch is closing," the attendant said, never lowering his weapon. "Please stand back."

The door began to lower, and Kholo gripped the arms harder, anticipating violence at any moment. But the hatch closed with no further argument from the enforcer. The attendant finally lowered his gun, and Kholo let out the breath he had held through the entire exchange. The attendant must have heard him as he turned toward Kholo and smiled. Tucking the gun into his robes, he came to Kholo's side.

"From your reaction, I take it you are the Banished they sought," the man said gently. Kholo nodded, staring up at him. The man smiled kindly. "Do not worry. We are heading for Simahla, and you are free, my friend."

The attendant patted Kholo's shoulder before moving on down the aisle. Kholo sat there in silence, repeating the man's words over and over in his mind.

I am free.

Ingozi's size had seemed so impossible when Kholo first brought his father in to seek treatment for his illness. But if Ingozi were a galaxy, then Simahla was the entire universe. He leaned across the still sleeping woman beside him to gaze out of the window in complete awe of the city's enormity. Even with how far above it they flew, it stretched beyond the horizon. But where Ingozi was cold, dark, and devoid of anything natural, here Kholo saw all manner of trees and plant life lining the streets and covering the rooftops. He understood perfectly why it was called the Emerald Sprawl.

"First time?" The sleeping woman said, snapping Kholo back to reality.

"Apologies," he said, leaning back into his own seat. The woman laughed as she straightened in her seat.

"No apology needed. But I do not think I have ever seen someone's eyes so big before," she said with a grin. "We all have that reaction our first time here. There is big, then there is Simahla big."

"It is unbelievable," Kholo whispered, casting his gaze back out the window.

The transit took them quite literally halfway around the world, and the entire trip lasted less than two hours. He chatted with his seat mate as they approached a transit center that looked as large as the entirety of Ingozi. The casting of the Great Working would occur that evening, and the atmosphere of the passengers turned jovial as they docked and prepared to disembark.

"What brings you to Simahla," the woman said as they walked down the ramp to the center proper.

"Freedom," Kholo said. The woman stopped; her eyebrows raised. Kholo stopped as well, and for a moment Kholo worried that he might have been mistaken to say anything at all. His worries melted away when the woman smiled.

"Then welcome home, brother," she said, surprising him by stepping up to him and wrapping her arms around him. He hesitated a moment before he hugged her in return. A screen winked to life in front of Kholo as the woman stepped back. It displayed a picture of the woman, as well as information about her line of work. He glanced to the actual woman who still grinned at him. "You will need an occupation now, and I can assist with that. After the Great Working, come find my company and we will make sure you can make a life for yourself here."

Tears gathered in his eyes as he stared at the information the woman had sent him. He whispered, "Thank you."

"We all thrive when we help each other," the woman said, starting off again down the ramp. "Freedom is to be enjoyed."

They parted when they entered the center, and she waved as she disappeared from view. The panic he had felt before started to creep back in, and he focused on the faces around me again, doing his best to keep his breathing even. He asked the neurolink to show him where the Satiras was in the city, and how long it might take him to walk there. Kholo's heart sank when he saw it took at least twelve hours travel on foot. He did not have enough credits left to hire a smaller transport to take him there.

"What should I do until tomorrow?" Kholo mused.

"Transports to the Satiras are free today," Fain answered. "I suggest finding one to take you as the Great Working will quite literally be a once in a lifetime event to see. Would you like me to book you passage?"

"Yes please," Kholo answered, his heart lifting. It only took seconds for Fain to secure a transport for him and he headed for the gate.

His second transport ride was much less enjoyable than the first. The hovercraft that picked Kholo up was the only one available for several hours, and it looked like it might fall apart at the slightest gust of wind. The ride itself did nothing to dispel that thought. The inside stank, and Kholo did his best not to think what might have made the stench. He never even saw the driver since they never lowered the dark partition.

They managed to reach the little station closest to the Satiras in one piece though, and the transport sped off the moment Kholo stepped out of it. With the number of trees and the grass growing around the pathways, the station looked more like a park. Kholo strolled from the station, glancing occasionally at the screen to the side that showed the map to his destination. He breathed deep, and though the stink of the transport may have skewed his opinion, he thought Simahla smelled surprisingly nice.

Even after leaving the station behind, all manner of foliage lined the walking paths that meandered through the buildings. Ropes of ivy sprawled across the glass and metal, and thick vines hung from the trees. It made for a much more pleasant walk than anywhere he had seen in Ingozi. The people here seemed much more friendly as well. Even though he had removed his wrap and his brand was in full view, they still looked him in the eye and smiled as he passed.

Kholo made it about halfway to the Sotiras when he started to encounter the crowds. It felt like a festival, with all manner of booths and carts selling so many different kinds of food and beverages that it boggled his mind. All of it smelled amazing, and his stomach grumbled a reminder of how long it had been since last he ate. He gazed at the carts longingly, but he had no credits to purchase with. One of the carts smelled particularly delicious, and he made a point to pass a little closer to it on his way. As he neared, he saw they served giant sausages on a skewer, their myriad glazes shining in the sunlight.

"Here friend!" the man at the cart said, holding out a sausage.

"Apologies, I have no credits," Kholo said, shaking his head sadly at the offered food. The man laughed.

"No credits needed. It is the casting day, so everyone deserves to celebrate," he said, pressing the sausage into Kholo's hand. He gave Kholo a good nature wave to shoo him on when he protested and turned to hand a sausage to the next person who stepped up.

His mother had always taught him to appreciate gifts from the Sisters, so Kholo sent up his thanks and bit into the sausage. The glaze was both spicy and sweet, and the meat itself was juicy beyond belief. The flavor that filled his mouth was unlike anything he had ever tasted, and he found his eyes tearing. Banished always had very limited access to spices and the like, and never honey which formed the base of the glaze. While his hunger demanded he eat the treat as fast as he could, Kholo instead forced himself to eat it slowly. Such pleasures had to be savored when they came.

As it turned out, it would not be the only pleasure he was allowed as he headed for the Sotiras. The celebrations only increased as he got closer, and the booths and stalls became even more generous. They handed him all manner of delicacies as he went, from luxurious meats to vegetables stuffed with cheeses and other tasty things, to wines and liquors and other drinks that set his belly on fire and left a smile on his face.

Kholo heard music of all kinds everywhere, some coming through speakers while others were played live. Women and men alike danced up to him, and he swayed and spun with them for a time before he moved on, and yet it always seemed like someone else waited to take their place. A group of children with a ball roped him into a game he did not know the rules of. But they laughed as he tried to decipher it and he found their mirth infectious. It should have only taken a half hour to reach the Sotiras' plaza; well before the casting at nightfall. But before he knew it, the shadows grew long as the Sisters dipped toward the horizon. But he had never enjoyed himself more.

At least until he heard the shouting.

It came from behind him, and Kholo glanced back to see what had caused the disruption. The sight of red and white set his heart racing. He put his head down and forced his way through the crowd, attempting to stay as unobtrusive as possible. The vendors still tried to press their treats on him, and others still tried to swing him into their dancing, but now he ignored them all. He did not know where he was going, only that he had to get away.

The Temple had been banned in Simahla, and the Banished freed. So why were there Temple Enforcers there? He knew instinctively that they searched for him. They were only an hour from sunset and the casting, though. Kholo just needed to stay hidden for a little longer.

The crush of people became quite literal as he passed into the plaza. Kholo did not even registered the people around him as he gazed up at the Sotiras. He had not expected the giant smooth, obsidian black sphere that dominated the center of the plaza. With the way it shone with the Sisters' waning light, it struck quite the impression.

A voice resonated from the Sotiras, making Kholo's bones quake. "Only one more needs to give their will to the Sotiras for the Great Working to be cast. If you have not done so, please step forward. The future of our world depends upon it."

"Allow me through, I have not given to the machine" Kholo said, pushing forward. The crowd around him gave curious looks his way. They carried his words along, and the people began to separate to give him a path.

"Stop him," someone called from behind. Kholo glanced back over his shoulder to see an enforcer pointing at him. Another five enforcers appeared, and the crowds scrambled to move out of their way as they rushed toward him. Kholo ran, shoving aside those that did not move fast enough. The crowd began to shout as well, and he glanced back to see that they had closed in around the enforcers. Strikers sparked, and men and women cried out in pain. But Kholo did not stop. No matter what, he needed to reach that obsidian sphere.

Expecting to feel hands on him at any moment, he managed to reach the barrier that kept the crowds back from the Sotiras. Soldiers patrolled the perimeter, and they raised their rifles when he approached.

"I wish to add my will, and I am being pursued" he shouted as he approached. The soldier glanced past him to the enforcers and nodded. He waved Kholo through, keeping his gun trained on the approaching enforcers. Kholo scrambled over the short barrier and broke into a run across the empty distance toward the sphere. A woman in clinical whites waved at him and pointed him to an opening in the sphere. He made a straight line as gunfire rang out across the plaza, drawing screams from the crowd.

Then a section of the ground in front of Kholo exploded. Bits of stone peppered him, staggering him and drawing blood. The ground exploded several more times around him as his pursuers continued to fire their gravity blasters. Now he knew how they had entered the theater in Ingozi. Kholo had seen a single shot from a gravity blaster blow a man in two. Panic pounded in his ears, and he tasted death as he ran. He prayed he would not die before he could forever escape death.

The Sisters ran with him, and he reached the opening bloodied but whole. Once inside, he turned as the woman fumbled to close the door and saw that the enforcers had only been a few steps behind. The man in front leveled a rifle at him and pulled the trigger just as the door closed. The bullet slammed into his belly, and he gasped as pain blossomed in his abdomen. The doors closed, and there was only silence.

Silence and the dark.

The dark swallowed Kholo whole, and only pain and his own ragged breathing existed around him. He pressed a hand to the wound in his belly, feeling the wetness of his blood on his skin. After only a few moments, a light flared into being, and he squinted at the sudden brightness. A screen had burst into life, and Kholo stumbled toward it. What looked like handprints sat on the far edges of it, and words scrawled down the center.

PLACE YOUR HANDS ON THE INDICATED PADS TO BEGIN TRANSFER OF WILL.

Gritting his teeth, Kholo removed his hand from his wound and placed both on the pads, his fingers splayed to match the print.

TRANSFER OF WILL TO BEGIN IN—3—2—1— START.

As soon as the countdown ended the pads heated rapidly beneath Kholo's palms. He tried to pull away, but he could not move in the slightest. The heat increased until he could no longer stand it, but he had lost his ability to scream. He could only stand and suffer.

Then the world shifted, and the chamber fell away.

Kholo stood on the scrub land that surrounded Ingozi. He pressed his hand into his belly, but he felt no pain, and when he looked there was no blood. He was whole again, though he did not know why. Turning, he saw his family's home behind him, exactly as he left it when he set out to carry his father into the city. The Sister suns watched from overhead, bathing Kholo in their warm light. A breeze tousled his robes, and he smiled at the pleasant sensation. It fled his lips as fast as it came though. How had he gotten here? And why?

"The Sotiras taps into your subconscious and scans for your reasons to live," a man said from beside Kholo, his voice deep and familiar. Uku-fa stepped into view, his eyes fixed on Kholo's family home. "The working is constructed of its subjects will to live, and those that add to it must have enough for the Sotiras to take without leaving them barren. It is meant to prevent death, not raise it."

"I am not here in actuality, then?" Kholo said. Ukufa shook his head.

"No, your awareness has been sent deep into your own subconscious. During both the scan and the transfer, the Sotiras shows you all the reasons to live on that you hold in your thoughts and memories."

"Then why show me this place?" Kholo said, turning his eyes back to the house. Or rather, the shack. His father could have built a far better home for them, but the people of Ingozi would not allow any of the Banished to have comfort of any kind. So, they had a shack that was not insulated, with boards that did not quite fit together and a roof that leaked. It was all they were allowed. The world over would consider living in such a way worse than the most violent prison they could think of, but as Kholo had told his father as he laid dying in his arms, he had been happy despite what the world thought.

"This structure was never my home," Kholo said, turning to find Ukufa watching him. "My family was. And they are gone. What would I have to return to here?"

"What, indeed. But the Sotiras has not been wrong yet. In your heart, the thought of returning to this place makes you want to continue on. Perhaps it is the promise you made to your father. That you would not die on the streets. Or perhaps you want to make it a home as bright and happy as it was with your family. The only person that can answer that question is you."

He strode toward the house and Kholo followed, pondering his words. A question nagged at his thoughts.

"Are you a construct of my subconscious as well?"

Ukufa halted, and after a moment he laughed, low and soft.

"I am very real."

"Then you are the real Ukufa?"

"I am, and I am not," he said with a small smile. Kholo had never seen anyone else wear the expression that shadowed Ukufa's face. Equal parts sadness, longing, hope, and an understanding of something Kholo knew by instinct laid far beyond his own comprehension. "There are parts of me in the story of Ukufa, He Who Holds Your Hand in Shadow. I have made my skin dark as the Shadow he coated his skin in to guide the newly deceased through the darkness to the Promised Tomorrow. But in reality, there is no Shadow to protect you from. It is one of my favorite interpretations of my existence I have encountered in the vast expanse of the universe, though. But while I do guide the spirits of the dead to the other side, Ukufa's story still does not truly describe my existence, but you may use the name if it pleases you. I quite enjoy it myself."

"Not Ukufa, but Death then," Kholo said. Ukufa nodded, looking up into the sky. "It does not take a great thinker to reason out why you are here on Etgaelna. But I would ask He Who Both is and is Not Ukufa, why he chooses to spend his time with me rather than anyone else on this planet."

"Since the first life ended in the universe and I blossomed into being, I have *known* things. It is how I *knew* both my purpose and how to carry it out. It is also how I *know* that there is no one else on this world more important than you."

Kholo blinked at him, utterly unsure of how to react. Ukufa laughed at his surprise and gestured for Kholo to follow as he continued on to the house. Kholo did so, and together they settled into the low chairs Kholo's father had crafted. Since he was a child, these chairs had always been Kholo's favorite. They were the one thing his father dared to craft well. They sat in silence for a time, enjoying the shade the little broken awning gave them as they watched the sparse grass sway in the wind.

"What makes me so important?" Kholo asked without tearing his gaze from the land.

"*That* I do not *know*," Ukufa said. "Only that you are."

"You both are and are not Ukufa, and now you both *know* and don't *know*." Kholo looked over to see him looking back, his eyebrow running for the top of his head. "Perhaps Contradiction might be a better name for you."

Ukufa started to laugh. Not a small laugh you give when humoring someone. It bubbled out of him like water from a freshly dug well. Kholo did not expect his joke to strike Ukufa as so amusing, but soon his own sides hurt with laughter. Then their eyes met, and they only laughed harder. It took a long time for either of them to be able to breathe properly again.

"That might be the most accurate description of me there is," Ukufa said as he wiped the tears from his eyes, a hint of laughter still lingering in his voice.

"I am happy I supplied it," Kholo said, still laughing himself.

Ukufa turned and grinned back at Kholo, and the sight took his breath away. Nothing Kholo had witnessed had ever been so beautiful. They slipped into silence for a time, and Kholo's thoughts gradually grew darker.

"You are here because I am dying," Kholo said finally.

"I am, though I do not yet *know* if you will."

"Then there is a chance I can still keep my promise to my father?" Kholo said, hopeful.

"There is," Ukufa said. "In reality you are bleeding out as the Sotiras gathers your will. The Great Working will be cast the moment the Sotiras has enough will. Whether that will happen before your body succumbs to your injury is still to be seen."

"Then we wait?" Kholo asked.

"We wait," Ukufa responded.

So they did.

They lapsed into silence again, and Kholo did not know how much time passed as they sat there watching the land. Eventually Kholo's vision began to waver. Suddenly panicked, he got to his feet.

"It seems the transfer is complete. The Sotiras won, and you will live," Ukufa said, standing as well. "And it is time for you to go. Thank you for the gift of my new name. If anyone deserves eternal life, it is you."

"Will I see you again?" Kholo said, his vision fading fast.

"If the Great Working succeeds, I imagine not," Ukufa said. He smiled at Kholo. "But I hope we do."

"So do I," Kholo said, smiling back. "And you should keep the name, Ukufa. It suits you."

Then the darkness took him.

TRANSFER COMPLETE. CASTING COMPLETE. WELCOME TO IMMORTALITY

Those words flared at Kholo as he came back to himself. He pulled his palms from the pads and stood straight. Expecting the skin of his palms to have burned to a cinder he inspected them. There was no sign of the overwhelming heat he had felt. Nor the blood that had covered them.

He felt no pain in his abdomen either, as he pressed his hands to his bullet wound. They came away red with fresh blood and anxiety crashed through his nervous system. Had the Great Working not worked on him? Was he still to die?

I will not die and there will be no pain, but my wound will bleed until the end of existence.

The thought ran unprompted through Kholo's mind. It came unbidden, but he knew beyond the shadow of a doubt it was true. How he knew this, he could not say. He thought then of the *knowings* that Ukufa had spoken of. Could this be the same?

The door to the chamber opened, letting in the dying light of the Sisters. He strode out onto the street, still pondering the *knowing* that had come to him.

The plaza held not a soul.

Kholo blinked, casting about for someone, anyone. He heard no music, no voices, even in the distance. Silence reigned absolute. Nothing moved as he made his way across the plaza. He left a trail of blood behind him, and it soaked his hand still held to the wound.

Darkness fell in full as Kholo wandered the streets searching for any sign of life. No matter how long he searched though, he found no one.

"Fain," he said, hoping he at least still had the AI. A screen winked to life before him, and he breathed a sigh of relief at the sight of her face.

"How can I assist you?"

"Do you detect any other neurolinks around us?" Kholo asked, though in the same instant he *knew* the answer.

"I do not pick up any other neurolink signals within my range."

"How wide is your range?"

"I can detect everything within the Simahla city borders."

That meant there was no one in the entirety of the city. Where could they have gone? He did not know. Standing there in the middle of the pathway, he drowned in the realization of what he did *know*.

There is no living person on the face of Etgael-na.

Versus Terminus
Part II

S tanding on a high walkway overlooking the largest Dark Matter Field Core ever devised by human hands, Professor Malik Devol pleaded with Head Engineer Adrienne Tenner for the future of humanity.

"It's going to fail, Adrienne," he said to the woman leaning against the railing opposite him. She regarded him with burnt umber eyes for a moment, then opened her mouth to say something. Malik didn't give her the chance. "Every simulation I've run has at least one of the DMFC's rings losing integrity and shutting down before our final Kerr wormhole transit."

To emphasize his point, Malik lifted his wrist and called up a holoscreen showing his most recent simulation. He ran the program, and it showed the DMFC running during the cradle ship's many treks through the wormholes created by entangled black holes on the way to the

Solis system that birthed their people. The system was over five hundred light years away and the wormholes were the only way they could cut down the transit time. The DMFC generated a tiny black hole of its own, and its gravitational pull gathered exotic matter around the ship like a shield to keep the wormhole open once entered, and keep the ship shielded from the extremely high-energy particles inside. If it failed in any way, the transit through the wormhole would rip the ship apart. As always, when the simulation reached the fifteenth and final transit, a message played across the screen.

CRITICAL FAILURE DETECTED. RING 5 COMPROMISED. FUNCTION AT 80%.

"I've run hundreds of sims, and every single one of them have roughly the same result," Malik said as the holoscreen winked out of existence.

"I understand your concerns, Devol," Adrienne said. She held up a hand as Malik started to argue. "I really do. But you must understand that only *your* sims have such unanimous results. Everything we've run shows only a six percent chance of a critical failure before the end of transit."

"That's because you're running those sims on the Saturn class systems," Malik said. He ran a hand through his hair in frustration, which was so disheveled you'd think he'd just been out in the storm constantly crashing against the biodome that housed the ship. "I'm running mine on the Salvator's Jupiter class system."

Adrienne heaved a long-suffering sign and turned to face him. "Devol, I'm not going to sit here and say the new AI system you created for the Salvator isn't a marvel, but it was made to monitor a cradle ship in a decades long voyage, not for this."

"But—"

"But," Adrienne said, cutting him off again. "The fact remains that you are not a certified DMFC engineer. I am. And every sim I've run puts the chance of critical failure at only six percent. And while that is higher than we'd like, it is within acceptable parameters given everything that is at stake here. We don't have time to re-engineer the whole thing at this point. Our window to get the Salvator off planet is closing quickly. This *will* work, Devol. It has to."

She put a hand on Malik's shoulder and gave him a slight smile.

"Have a little faith."

A rush of anger welled up in his chest at that, and Malik shoved it down. He brushed her hand from his shoulder and said, "It will take more than faith to deliver us safely to the Solis system."

"Devol—"

"Thank you for listening to my concerns, Head Engineer Tenner," he said before she could try to reason with him further, opting for formality to ensure he stayed civil. "If you will excuse me, I have matters to attend to."

"Of course," Adrienne said, seeming confused by his sudden change in demeanor.

Malik turned on his heel and headed for the exit to the Core bay. The eyes of the engineers working on the DMFC followed him as he went, but he didn't look their way. They thought him crazy, he knew. For the smartest engineers left on Terra Secundo, they were all far too damn stupid. Adrienne was correct in that he wasn't a DMFC engineer. And while he might not know the entire process of building one, as an AI and robotics engineer, he knew a thing or two about structural integrity, and it was simple to obtain the operating data for a Core. All he did was apply the material and size data for the Salvator's core to the standard stress test sim.

The only difference was Jupiter was far smarter than Saturn, and it could account for far more variables. That they wouldn't even take his data into account was tantamount to criminal negligence.

I'm not going to let a black hole crush humanity to a singularity because some engineers are too proud to admit they might be wrong, he thought angrily to himself.

As he left the bay behind, a woman standing at the far end of the corridor caught his eye and made the air freeze in his lungs. The face he looked at was so painfully familiar, and so impossible in its presence. She watched him for several seconds before turning and walking out of sight. Malik started forward but he stopped himself just before he broke into a run.

Anaisha can't be here, he thought, shaking his head. *My sister is dead, and I can't go chasing ghosts.*

It took Malik over an hour to travel from the DMFC bay to the ship's protected entrance. A myriad of droids sped about the halls, some carrying materials, some finishing up various wiring and paneling that still needed doing. And everywhere the Mars class droids—generally called Annihilators for reasons easy to guess—stood watch. The fact that the giant, hulking things floated across the floor always unsettled Malik. They looked like burly, barrel-chested power lifters, gigantic arms and all. Of course, their arms were that big to house the lasers, blades, and explosives the battle droids would use to keep the Mundi safe.

When he disembarked, he took a moment to look back at the ship. The Salvator Mundi—the Savior of the World—wasn't just a space vessel. It was a flying city. Twelve miles long and nearly three miles at its widest, it dwarfed anything that humanity had built in the past. It was meant to carry roughly fourteen thousand people out of the Vox Humanitas system. An unfortunately small amount compared to the eight hundred million humans left on Terra Secundo. While he gazed at the ship, the ground beneath him shook and Malik lost his balance, falling to his knees.

The tremors are getting more frequent, he thought, that constant anxiety he'd had for years now surging to the front of his mind. *The planet won't last much longer.*

He got his feet under him again and headed for the transport that waited to take him home. A year ago, he would have walked, but Terra Secundo's storms had become it's storm. Singular. And it hadn't abated in the last four months. Unless you had a space worthy suit, it was too dangerous to venture out into it, and even then, survival wasn't guaranteed.

Mining made Terra Secundo seismically unstable just like every other terrestrial planet, moon, and asteroid in the entire system. At Malik's birth, nineteen billion humans inhabited the various planets and colonies across the system. But nineteen billion people require an overwhelming amount of resources to sustain. Seventy-five percent of the viable material in the system had been mined already when Malik entered the universe. In just over forty years they'd mined the rest.

The off-world settlements died first. The first resource to run dry was fuel. Humanity should have abandoned fossil fuels centuries ago, but with planetary mining giving them an abundance of fossil material and the development of atmospheric filtration systems, they'd continued the use. But when they began to run out of fuel, Vox Gov began to ration it. The far-flung colonies lost access first, and no longer able to receive supply shipments or leave the colony they began to die. One by one they collapsed, and the people either starved to death, or killed each other just to live another day.

When Terra Prime became uninhabitable, Malik knew they'd sealed their fate. It was one of only two planets that were naturally fit for life in the system, and the only one that had a rotation. It had also been the richest in some of the crucial materials to space travel, and they'd mined it until there was barely anything left of the planet in the planet.

Now, with ninety-six percent of humanity dead, tidally locked Terra Secundo was all they had left.

Malik stared out at the rain pummeling the streets through the hovercraft's window. The storm raged so densely that he could see barely anything of Ring City. Though the constant twilight he remembered from when he was a boy had always made it feel like time never moved in the City that Surrounds the World, he much preferred it over the persistent darkness of the Storm.

The raging winds made the hovercraft lurch and shake the entire way to his living quarters, and Malik maintained a death grip on his protective restraints. He always worried the Storm would make the scanning tech the hovercraft used to "see" malfunction, and he'd imagined his transport slamming into the side of a building, or into another craft, a million times. The hovercraft beat the odds again and delivered him to his quarters shaken but unscathed.

"I'm back," he called out, closing the door to his quarters behind him. Footsteps padded toward him from the main room as he shrugged off the white coat that designated him as one of the Salvator's head engineers. He hung it on the rack and turned to the woman who'd just entered the entryway.

"How did it go?" she said, her voice full of equal parts hope and worry.

"She still wouldn't listen," he said, shaking his head. The woman's face fell.

"What are you going to do now?" she asked. Malik opened his mouth to speak, and his stomach did so for him. The woman laughed.

"Looks like your stomach doesn't care that humanity is about to end," she said, starting back toward the main room and gesturing for him to follow. "Come on, I made you some dinner."

"Thank you, 3:56," he said, following the android.

Android model 3, version 56 amazed him every time he saw her. Malik pushed the boundaries of AI his entire life, and as amazing as everyone thought the Jupiter Class system was that he'd created for the Mundi, it was nothing next to 3:56. With the advances in synthetic skin and bionic organs, she looked and felt like a living human, but she *felt* in a way no other robot ever had. When she smiled, it reached her eyes. There was real joy there. The same when something saddened her and the corners of her mouth turned down in the barest hint of a frown. She wrinkled her nose when she smelled something she disliked, and she had a way of pursing her lips when deep in thought. She possessed all the unique little quirks and mannerisms that made any person themselves, and they came naturally as her personality developed.

He had matched the darkness of her skin, the curls of her hair, and the emerald of her eyes to his own. If she looked like his family, then no one would ask questions about her. But he hadn't intended for her to look so much like his sister when they were young, or how much guilt the thought would bring him. Because he felt like he'd subconsciously tried to replace his sister. And because 3:56 herself didn't deserve to be someone else's stand in.

3:56 placed a plate of naan and a bowl of lentil soup in front of him. It wasn't much, but most in Ring City would consider it a feast at this point. 3:56 watched as he began to eat, a small smile playing about her lips. How she was able to make her cooking taste just like his mother's he still didn't know.

"It's delicious as always," he said, smiling back at her. "Did you not make any for yourself?"

"You know I don't *need* to eat," she said, gesturing for him to continue. "I just can. Rations are dwindling, and we can't afford to waste the little that we get."

"True, but life still has to be worth living," Malik said, picking up a spoonful of soup and holding it out toward her. "Here, at least have a taste."

3:56 blinked at the spoon and looked up at Malik with uncertain eyes.

"Really, I'm—"

"I insist."

She scrunched up her face, obviously torn as to what to do, and Malik brought the spoon a little closer to her face. She huffed a laugh and took the bite. Malik watched her savor the flavor of the soup for a moment before continuing to eat himself.

"You said there would be something for us to talk about if the head engineer still wouldn't listen," 3:56 said when she finally swallowed the spoonful of soup. Malik froze. "She didn't listen, so what did you want to talk about?"

Malik had hoped she would at least wait until after he finished eating to bring up what he told her before he left that morning. But he couldn't blame her, she must have thought about it all day after all. He wiped up the last of the soup with a piece of naan and popped it in his mouth as he thought about just what he was about to ask of her.

"You've run the same sims as I have," he said, putting his elbows on the table and resting his chin on the backs of his hands. "So you know as well as I do that the Mundi's DMFC isn't going to hold up for the entire trek."

She nodded; her face serious.

"Tenner won't budge, and I can't do the work needed to put the safeguards in place alone. Even if I tried, Jupiter would alert her and the other leads immediately." He chuckled. "I did my job a little too well there."

"What can I do to help?" 3:56 said, leaning across the table, determination in her eyes. Malik clenched his teeth. He knew that she would agree to anything he asked of her, especially for something like this. And he hated what kind of person it made him that he was going to ask her anyway.

"The DMFC *will* lose functionality in some way before the end. And if I can't get *them* to put additional contingencies in place, then I will," Malik said, not able to look at her as he spoke. "The only thing I can do is make sure there is someone that knows how to repair the Core when it finally breaks. I'd do it myself, but—"

"But," she said, making Malik look up at her. "All of our projections show the issues occurring eighty to a hundred years into the voyage, and not only would you not survive the journey, but you would more than likely already be gone when the Core malfunctions."

She brought her feet up onto her chair and wrapped her arms around her legs.

"But I will."

"Yes," Malik said, feeling like someone had a vice grip on his stomach. "I know how selfish it is of me to ask this of you, but I have to. You're the only person that can ensure humanity survives."

He cast his eyes down into his lap, his vision blurring with tears.

"I hate myself for putting this on your shoulders. Jupiter will do everything in its power to destroy you if it detects you. You don't deserve decades of isolation and constantly being hunted. Just because you *can* do this doesn't mean you should have to, and I—"

Arms wrapped around Malik's neck, startling him. 3:56 had moved behind him and she hugged him tight, nuzzling her cheek against his.

"Please don't cry," she said softly into his ear. "I've known all along that it would come to this. And I'm going to do it because I want to, and for no other reason. But I appreciate how much you care about a robot."

"Not just a robot," Malik said, reaching up and placing a hand on her arm and feeling the warmth of her synthetic skin. "You're as alive as any human. You're also the only family I have, and I'll protect any of my loved ones with my life. So I hate myself for asking you to give up so much of yours."

"Family…" 3:56 whispered. Malik felt moisture on his cheek as she hugged him tighter.

"Family," Malik said, squeezing her arm.

She let him go and stepped back. Malik turned and stood as she wiped her eyes, grinning all the while. He couldn't help but grin back. When he made her, he never imagined she'd become so close and so important to him. But he'd meant every word. She *was* family. The daughter he never had.

"What's the plan?" 3:56 said when her tears had dried. "How am I going to be the Salvator's savior?"

The notification came only seconds before they walked out into the larger hall. Malik jumped back, pulling 3:56 with him. They slipped into a gap between coolant pipes just in time to avoid the Annihilator's scan. Malik held his breath, fighting hard to keep from moving in any way. 3:56 closed her eyes and stilled completely. It wasn't often that the fact she wasn't human surfaced, but it did now, and Malik fought down the shudder at the sudden uncanny valley.

The Annihilator floated by their hiding place, the hiss of its propulsion jets echoing along the steel of the Salvator's walls. It slowed for a moment in front of the opening, and Malik's heart beat a frantic pace as he waited for death. The droid continued on, disappearing down the corridor. Malik counted to ten before letting out the breath he held. 3:56 opened her eyes when he did.

"A little too close," he said, giving her a crooked grin.

"Why did you not get the notification earlier?" she asked, concern in her eyes.

"I can only access Jupiter so much without the system's safeguards discovering the breach and sending every droid on board to wipe us out of existence," Malik said, shimmying toward the opening to peek out. Neither the Annihilator nor any other kind of bot lingered in the corridor. "I can only ping the system every so often, and only for a second or two. We've got to be careful, because I can't guarantee we'll have any kind of warning before we've got an Annihilator on us."

"I'll be careful," 3:56 said. Malik was grateful for the determination in her voice.

They slid out into the corridor, staying close to the wall as they hurried along. They strained their ears for any sign of droids. If they encountered one, it wouldn't matter if it was a Mars droid or not. All the other classes were programmed to report any anomalous presence to Jupiter for assessment. A Vulcan repair bot would have a dozen Annihilators on them within seconds.

The DMFC bay rested in the center of the Salvator to better distribute the dark matter it collected around the ship. Vox Gov only allowed one entrance to be accessible at a time to ensure only authorized personnel could board. A necessary precaution with the hordes of people either trying to stow away or sabotage the whole thing. He understood both. Only fourteen thousand would make the journey to the

Solis system, barely over one percent of their remaining population, so he understood the resentment of those who would die on Terra Secundo.

Every time he looked away from a parent begging him to give their children passage, he hated himself more. Malik shook his head. Only fourteen thousand would make the trip, but without 3:56 in place, even *they* wouldn't survive. Humanity having any kind of future depended on her.

"Does it seem too quiet to you?" 3:56 asked while Malik worked to bypass the biometric lock on an auxiliary passage that led down to the DMFC's floor. He paused, listening. She was right. There should still be bots working on various final projects throughout this section, and with the Salvator's design, he should hear *something*.

But there was only quiet.

"Yes," he said, quickening his pace on the lock. "We can't take the time to investigate, though. If anything, it might give us a better chance at success."

3:56 didn't respond, and Malik could feel her dissatisfaction. The lock beeped and the door slid open. She frowned when he turned to her, and he sighed as she stepped by without a word.

"I promise you I will check into it once you're settled," he said to her back. "But our mission is more important."

She stopped, and after a moment she sighed herself.

"I know," she said, giving him a worried smile over her shoulder. "I just have a bad feeling."

He didn't say it, but so did he.

Three levels and a dozen bypassed biolocks later, and Malik's worry had quickly become alarm. They hadn't seen a single bot the entire time, not even one of the small cleaners. One could only manufacture that kind of luck, and Malik knew something was going on. Something bad. But no matter how many concerned looks 3:56 shot him, he held his tongue.

The engineering deck was purely operational and not meant for passengers, ergo the halls were much smaller, making the level feel claustrophobic. They sneaked through the passages toward the droid bay 3:56 would occupy for the duration of the transit. Not that they needed to, though. They didn't catch so much as a glimpse of anything else on the deck, and Malik fought to keep his breathing under control. Having a panic attack now wouldn't help anything.

"This is it," 3:56 said, peeking around the corner at the entrance to the bay. They had worried too many droids would be moving through the area for her to make it into the hideaway bay. Malik now wished that was the case. He placed a hand on 3:56's shoulder.

"We made it," he said, painting on a grin and forcing his voice to remain even. "We're lucky you can get in there without a fight."

"There's something going on." She held up a hand as Malik started to speak. "Don't lie to me, I know what the lack of droid presence means as well as you."

"3:56—"

"I know what I need to do, and that I can't abandon that to go with you," she said, cutting him off again. "I'm going to be in that little room for a century, and the only way I'm going to make it through is if I know you'll be waiting for me on the other side."

She gave him a little punch to the arm, her expression so serious that Malik couldn't help the tears that gathered in his eyes. She was going to spend a century locked inside a droid bay because he couldn't convince Tenner and the others they were wrong.

"I'm sorry," he said, his voice breaking. "I'm sorry you're doing this because of me."

She reached up and wiped away the tear trickling down his face with her thumb.

"Not *because* of you," she said with a smile. "For you. You've protected me since the moment I opened my eyes, keeping me safe from those that would only see me as something to destroy so they could recreate my technology."

She wrapped her arms around him and buried her face in his chest.

"I'm going to protect you this time," she said, her words muffled.

Malik smiled and hugged his daughter tight.

"I've got to go," he said reluctantly. 3:56 nodded and stepped back. Without a word she turned and hurried to the hideaway bay. The hatch opened at her touch and she ducked inside. She looked out again as the hatch began to close.

"I'll see you later, professor."

The hatch hissed as it sealed her in.

"I'll see you later," Malik said, waving back at her even though he knew she couldn't see it. "I promise."

He held up his wrist and a holoscreen flared to life. Accessing Jupiter from his personal unit was risky. He put the safeguards in place himself after all, and he knew if he poked around too much, it would poke back. But even a hint of a threat to the Salvator made the risk worth it.

It didn't take long for him to bypass the security measures and log onto Jupiter. Working as fast as he could, he ran a droid status report for the ship so he could see all their current positions. That 3:56 didn't show up gave him relief. The lack of any other droid on the engineering deck made that relief short lived. His certainty that someone caused this solidified, and their motivation had to be malicious. He ran another scan for organic life on the deck, and came back with nothing, not even himself. Someone had jammed the signals. Yeah, definitely malicious.

His first thought was the DMFC. It was essential to their transits after all. He quickly discounted it though. Other than the heavy stress of the wormhole jumps, it would be extremely hard to damage its thick tungsten rings, and even harder to disassemble without an egregious amount of time. That meant they were after the engines at the aft of the ship. He'd never been athletic, so on foot it would take him far too long to reach them, and since the passengers would be in cryo for the journey, the designers had foregone tram systems, and they'd instead relied on—

"Wheelers," he said aloud, feeling stupid for not thinking of them first. Then again, the small electric transports had never been available to ferry him around the ship since he'd become non-essential personnel until take-off after he'd completed Jupiter's installation. He ran a hasty search and found one available close by. Hoping that he'd gone undetected, he logged out of Jupiter and raced toward the wheeler.

Having never driven a wheeler before, it took Malik longer to reach the engine bay than it should, but still far quicker than if he'd been on foot. Why they hadn't made them self-driving, he didn't know. He left the vehicle behind a small distance from the bay itself, not wanting to alert anyone to his presence before he could assess the situation.

He slipped through the entrance to the bay without encountering anyone or anything. Once inside, he could make out the faint murmur of voices in the distance, and he quickened his pace while trying to stay as quiet as possible. The voices grew louder as he neared the engine bay itself, and he started to pick out the sounds of tools as well. Any thought of staying quiet left his mind at that, and he ran full tilt down the corridor.

The observation room was surprisingly empty when Malik crept inside. He moved to the corner of the huge window that overlooked the engines and peaked out. The amount of people in the bay stabbed anxiety through him down to the marrow. Near a hundred hurried about, all working at the engines with frightening precision. How they got this equipment here defied Malik's understanding. He expected maybe a handful, and while he was no fighter, he thought he could figure out a way to stop a small group. But what could he do about this many?

He slid to the ground to keep out of sight and leaned against the window. This was no military ship with entire armories of weapons he might use to handle this. In fact, weapons of any kind were strictly prohibited aboard the Salvator, save for the Annihilators. Malik looked up and smiled. He didn't need a weapon. He just needed the Annihilators to do their job.

The holoscreen flared to life again when he held up his wrist, and he hurriedly bypassed the systems again to log into Jupiter. This time he didn't worry about Jupiter finding him. In fact, he intended it to. A new scan showed that while they'd been banished from the engineering deck, this deck's Annihilators had grouped around the closest path back down. Jupiter was entirely aware of this group's interference, and it just waited until it could break whatever program was blocking it.

Malik dove into Jupiter's back end processes to see its progress in breaking the block. It worked at an unbelievable pace, but this blocking system the group had uploaded into Jupiter was a masterpiece on its own. Powered by its own AI, Jupiter not only had to break its coding, but it had to fight against the AI undoing its work in real time. He had total confidence that

Jupiter would overcome this program, but it would be too late to save the engines.

Why the hell isn't someone capable of making a program like this part of the Salvator's team?

It took a few minutes, but Malik quickly got a grasp on how this new system worked, and what Jupiter was doing to undo it. He launched into the fray himself, fighting the program alongside Jupiter. The work was difficult, especially on a personal unit, but their combined effort gained ground quickly. It was obvious that they'd not expected a third party to aid Jupiter since the program's AI ignored Malik completely.

Thirty minutes later the program finally gave up the ghost and they purged its presence from Jupiter's systems. Malik ran several hurried scans while Jupiter was occupied with its final checks for the malicious program. The Annihilators rocketed into motion the second the block ended, and they would descend on the engine bay in a matter of moments.

He input his credentials to take himself off their scrub list, no longer worried about the other engineers knowing about his presence and lifted up enough to look down onto the bay floor to see the men and women continuing on in their work with no change. They must not know their program had been taken down.

A woman in the crush turned and looked up at him. Her emerald eyes met his, and his chest ached. He'd discounted it the first time he saw her. It was impossible after all. But here she was again. Why?

"Anaisha," he whispered, placing a hand on the glass.

The door to the observation room hissed open and a bullet slammed into Malik's back before he could even glance back. Another two followed it, and he fell. The stamp of boots approached, and someone flipped him over and shoved the muzzle of a rifle into his face.

"I'll be damned. It's Devol," a rough voice said. Malik looked up into the eyes of the woman in military darks holding the gun. "Why are you on the ship?"

He tried to answer, but he couldn't draw a breath to get the words out. The shots must have punctured his lungs.

"It doesn't matter," a man said from somewhere around him. "He's dead anyway."

The door to the room hissed open again and the two screamed as a concentrated laser cut through the room. It cut the woman with the gun in half, and the rifle smashed into Malik's face as she toppled over. He caught a glimpse of the Annihilator floating over him before his vision tunneled into darkness.

I'm sorry, 3:56, he thought as he slipped away.

There were a myriad of things Malik expected to experience in his life, but looking down at his own corpse had never passed his mind as possible, much less probable. Yet, here he stood, staring down at himself and the pool of blood that surrounded him. The Annihilator hovered beside his body for a few moments before turning and moving back toward the door.

"This must be a jarring moment for you."

Malik looked up at the woman who'd spoken from the doorway and the ache in his chest returned.

"Anaisha," he said. His sister smiled when he said her name and walked through the door toward him.

"I'm sorry, Malik," she said, her tone tender. "But I'm not your sister."

"You have to be," he said, watching her approach. "You look just like—"

"Just like she did the day she died," she said as she stopped in front of him. She raised a hand and placed it on his cheek. "Your heart has yearned for this for so long, and while I am only an image of her, I wished to give you some measure of happiness."

Malik reached up and placed his hand over hers. He wanted so badly for this to be Anaisha, but now that he looked into her eyes up close, he knew what she said was true. They were still the same brilliant emerald, but their eldritch depths told him whoever this woman was, she wasn't human. No mortal thing could know the things her eyes said she knew.

"If you aren't Anaisha, then who are you?"

Her fingers slipped from his face, and she turned her back to him.

"I've had many names. Thanatos. Anubis. Supay. Hel. Mania. Mors." She fell silent for a moment before saying, "Ukufa."

She faced him once more.

"In the dark ages of humanity, they called me the Grim Reaper. I don't believe any of these truly describe my existence, but you may call me what you will."

"Are you telling me that you're Death?"

"If you wish to think of me as such. But that's not quite correct. Death is a natural part of existence. All life ends, and I have no say in its happening. I'm just a guide."

"A guide to what?"

"To what is next."

Malik looked down at his body and shivered.

"So you're here to take me there?"

"I don't *know* yet," she said, something odd in her tone. Confusion perhaps? "It's a rare thing for me not to *know* if I am to open the door for you."

Malik looked up and the ache in his chest deepened at the sight of this woman who his eyes said should be his sister.

"Can you not look like her?" he snapped, gritting his teeth. A gentle smile graced her face.

"Of course. I don't wish to cause you undue pain. What form would you like me to take?"

"I don't care," he said, looking down at his body again, preferring to see himself deceased than this lie of his sister. "Just not her."

"Does this suit you?" said a deep voice, making Malik look up.

The man before him had skin so dark, Malik thought he'd see the twinkling of stars if he looked close enough. He looked at Malik with eyes like galaxies, and Malik had to fight to keep from losing himself among them. The grey and white robes he wore stood in stark contrast to his visage and seemed odd against the perfection of his form.

All doubt that this was Death fled from Malik's mind.

"You are the most beautiful thing I have ever seen," Malik managed to say. Death gifted him a sunrise of a smile.

"In all the long eons I have walked the universe, you are the first to say that to me," Death said with a laugh. "It always surprises me that there are still firsts I can experience."

"If you aren't here to take me, then why *are* you here?" Malik said, wrestling himself back under control.

"I have watched this system for some time," Death said, his smile vanishing. "Your people have died at a rate seldom seen, and I have found myself here more often than not."

Death walked to the observation window and placed a hand on the glass as he looked down. Malik looked as well and immediately wished he hadn't. Three Annihilators floated around the engine bay now littered with the mangled and dismembered corpses of the saboteurs. Malik hadn't even heard them die.

"There are more humans in the universe than any other intelligent species," Death said, his tone distant. "I do not know why. Perhaps you are the most suited vessels for life. Or maybe your bodies are just the easiest for the universe to make. In any case, there are trillions upon trillions of humans all throughout existence. And more often than not, your civilizations end up just like this."

Death tore his gaze away from the dead below and fixed it on Malik.

"Neither of the other two species that have achieved intergalactic travel consume worlds the way you do. And it makes me wonder if your species should exist at all."

The lack of emotion in Death's voice chilled Malik to the bone, but he felt that Death wanted something from him, though he didn't know what.

"I've had the same thought," Malik said, meeting Death's eldritch eyes. "The entire time I developed Jupiter, I constantly wondered if I should. Fourteen thousand are going to leave the Vox Humanitas system, and I'd be lying if I said I wasn't afraid this exact same thing will happen again. I know we're parasites. We move into a host system until we eat it from the inside out and move on to the next. I've wanted to walk away from the Salvator more times that I can count."

"Why have you not?"

Malik grinned as 3:56 swam through his mind.

"Because I have someone I want to protect."

Death nodded.

"The android."

"The android," Malik agreed, closing his eyes. "I don't care if a single person in this system survives. I just want her to be safe."

"What is it about her that gives you such motivation?"

Another easy answer.

"All of the other Class 3 droids I've created have disappeared, so I designed her to be similar enough in appearance to me that it would be easy to believe that we are related should we be seen together," Malik said. "I did it to keep her safe while she assisted me. But she's more human than I ever thought possible, and she's become more than just my invention.

Malik opened his eyes and wiped away the tears that had gathered.

"She's my daughter."

"She is still just an android though. A facsimile of life that will never be real," Death said in that same emotionless voice. Malik's feeling that Death wanted something from him strengthened.

"She is far more than just an android, and she is very much alive," Malik said with a shake of his head. "I've designed androids my entire life and the most advanced units there are came from my labs and my AI. But no matter how well made, none of them could ever be mistaken for human. They're good actors, but you can always tell that their emotions are algorithmic, and their movement is never exactly right. But not 3:56. The moment she opened her eyes for the first time, I could not see her as anything other than human."

Malik remembered how her eyes had fluttered open like someone waking from a deep sleep rather than the unnatural snap open every other android did when their systems came online.

"Do you know what it is that tells me that she's truly alive?" Malik asked.

"I do not," Death said, a hint of something finally coloring his voice. Hope?

"I made her the exact same way I made every other android in her line. There is absolutely *nothing* different about her design, or the build process. *She* is different. I made the body and the brain, but she provided the soul."

"She provided the soul..."

Death said the words as if he were trying them on, hoping they would fit. He turned in the direction of the DMFC and the bay 3:56 was in, his brow furrowed.

"I never had any idea how all of this would end," Malik said. "But every time I looked into her eyes, all of my anxiety vanished, and I knew that what would be on the other side of all of this might not be what I expected, but it will be far better than I feared."

"I like that," Death said. "I like that very much. You are also correct."

Death turned back to Malik, his eyes sparkling with wonder.

"She does indeed have a soul."

Every thought in Malik's mind fled save one. 3:56 *has a soul.*

"How?" he managed to say.

"I do not know," Death said, his voice filled with an emotion that Malik didn't understand. "But it is there, and it is so bright. How you managed to give her true life, I suspect we will never know. But you did."

"3:56 has a soul," Malik whispered aloud this time, grinning like a child.

"And yet another first," Death said, grinning along with him. "A question, though. Why have you never given her a name?"

"I've always called the androids I create by their model generation and number," Malik said. "She asked me to give her one, but she'd fully become her own person by then, and I wanted her to find her own name. She may be my daughter, but she's never been a child, and I wanted her to pick a name for herself that felt right."

Malik ran his hand through his scruffy hair, a wave of guilt crashing into him.

"The only argument we've ever had was over it, actually. Looking at it now, I feel stupid. Of course she'd want her father to name her. Why did I fight her so hard over it?"

Death's hand settled onto Malik's shoulder, surprising him. Suddenly afraid, Malik's head snapped up to the man, only to find the man gazing gently back.

"Do not worry, you will have another chance," Death said, squeezing his shoulder. "Do not waste it."

"What chance will I have?" Malik said, looking back down at his body, only to find it gone. Only the pool of his blood remained. "Where did it go?"

Death squeezed Malik's shoulder, and the world around them twisted. When everything came into focus again, they were in a hospital. The recovery pod in the center of the room gave off a soft green glow, revealing Malik's body inside.

"When did we get here?" Malik said, bewildered. He pointed at the pod. "When did I get here?"

"They recovered you while we spoke," Death said. "Time often passes differently on this level of existence. I have blinked and found that a thousand stars had died during the act. Other times a single second has lasted an eon."

"Am I not going to die?" Malik asked, his eyes fixed on his own face in the pod.

"You are not, though you came very, very close. It is why I was able to speak with you like this," Death said, walking up to the pod and placing his hand on the glass. The door behind them hissed open, and a group of doctors and nurses bustled in, followed by Tenner. Her face full of concern caught Malik entirely by surprise. She walked up to the pod and placed her hand on it in an almost perfect reflection of Death as the medical team got to work around them.

"Our time has come to an end," Death said, stepping back. "Thank you for answering my questions."

"You're welcome, though I don't know how much use my answers were to you."

"More than you know," Death said, placing his hand on Malik's shoulder again. "Go now and live for your daughter. And when you see her again, make sure you give her the name she deserves."

Malik's eyes fluttered open as the recovery pod drained. Tenner's face swam into view, her expression pure relief that he was awake.

"Welcome back," she said as the nurses worked to unhook him from the pod. "I didn't think you were going to make it there for a minute."

"Neither did I," Malik said, looking up at the ceiling above him. The nurses removed the last IV and he sat up slowly, the ache in his back making it hard to move.

"If you hadn't been there, the Salvator wouldn't be leaving today," Tenner said, placing a hand on his back to steady him. He flinched at her touch, making her do so in turn.

"I've been in here a week?" Malik asked, bewildered. He knew that his conversation with Death had lasted longer than he thought, but that was far outside anything he expected.

"You have, and you're incredibly lucky to have woken up," Tenner said, holding him up along with the other nurses so he could step out of the pod. "You had no vitals when we found you, and in all honesty, we didn't expect the pod to actually work. And even when it did, we never expected you to regain consciousness in time to be transferred to your cryo chamber. Yet here we are with you having surpassed all of my expectations."

"You didn't think I'd go through all of this just to watch you take off without me, did you?" he said, wincing as his feet touched the floor. He stumbled a bit as he gained his balance, but he didn't fall. "I made a promise, after all."

"To who?" Tenner said, curious.

"The most important person in the world."

Malik was cleared by the Mundi's medical team within the hour, and Tenner herself drove him to the cryo deck. Neither talked on the way, and the emptiness of the decks made his back ache harder. He knew the droids were supposed to be tucked away in their bays this time, but he felt uneasy regardless. When they reached the lift that would take them up to the cryo deck, Tenner parked the wheeler.

"We're going on foot from here," she said as she got out. "We've got fourteen thousand up there all heading for their own chambers and clogging the way."

They loaded into the lift, and Malik leaned against the wall as Tenner input the command. She looked back at him as the lift began to move, suspicion painted on her face.

"I'm glad you managed to stop the sabotage effort, but why were you on board?" she said, making Malik stiffen.

"I caught wind of the sabotage plot at the last minute, so I decided—"

Tenner slammed a hand into the wall next to Malik's face, making him jump. She brought her face close to his, her eyes like steel.

"Don't lie to me," she said through gritted teeth. "I checked Jupiter's access records. You logged in twice from your personal unit using bypasses. You also went to the DMFC bay before you went to the engines. There was no maintenance or checks for you to run, and no reason for you to be on board. So, tell me why you were."

Malik straightened as best he could and glared back into Tenner's eyes.

"And if I don't?"

"Then you won't make it to your chamber," Tenner spat.

"Yes. I will," Malik said, never breaking his gaze. "You cannot afford me not to make this transit."

"Malik—"

"I was here to do what you wouldn't," Malik said, cutting her off. "The DMFC *will* fail before we reach the Solis system, and I've put safeguards in place to ensure we survive this journey."

"The DMFC will not fail, and we *will* arrive at Terra without issue," Tenner said, but her words lacked conviction. She knew he was right. In fact, Malik imagined she'd known all along. But it had been too late to change the design or make egregious alterations. So they'd ignored his data and hoped their own was correct.

"You are correct about the latter, at least," Malik said, putting a hand on Tenner's shoulder and pushing her back. "I have ensured it."

"What did you do?"

"I doesn't matter, because there is no time to change anything at all now."

The doors to the lift opened, and the roar of a crowd spilled in. Malik slipped by Tenner and onto the deck. He turned back to her and grinned.

"Get to your chamber, Head Engineer Tenner. You'll thank me when we get there."

He staggered into the crowd heading for their own chambers, leaving Tenner behind. He didn't pay attention to those around him. If he looked into their faces, he'd just see the thousands more that wouldn't make it off the planet.

His back was pure agony when he finally reached his chamber. He'd checked several times, thinking maybe the wounds had reopened. But not only did he find no blood, he could find no trace of the bullet holes. But the agony persisted, nonetheless. He placed a hand on the biometric pad and the doors slid open. It took immense effort for him to maneuver into place for the cryo process to start, and all the strength left him when he finally did.

The doors slid shut and everything went quiet. He reached out and typed in his transit code on the little screen to the side. It flashed an acceptance and started the bio scan to confirm his identity. Once done, the chamber began to chill rapidly. Knowing what came next, Malik grit his teeth. Even still, he screamed when a thousand needles stabbed into him. It took everything he had to keep himself still as the sedation and preservation processes began.

Within seconds, the world began to fade. An image of 3:56 flashed before him, and Malik smiled. *I'll see you soon,* he thought as the darkness took him.

Salvator 3:56

Part III

D estruction came without feeling.

Android 3:56 had felt the first bite of the Mars Class security droid's laser; the fabricated nerves the Professor laced through her synthetic skin saw to that. She had almost reached the Dark Matter Field Core to start her repairs when it burned through her. When she tried to run the second Annihilator severed her legs. She remembered the jolt of pain when her head slammed into the floor as she fell. Then the coolness of the metal on her cheek.

But in the end, destruction came without feeling.

Death was made for flesh and blood and bone. For the natural. Androids didn't die. If something damaged their circuitry, they ceased to function, or were decommissioned. They could be turned off, re-purposed, or destroyed. But they did not die. And they did not pass on to some other level of existence. No, that was re-served for the humans and the "souls" they so fervently believed in.

What has happened to me, then? 3:56 won-dered as she stared down at her broken and twisted shell.

A laser blast through the chest had destroyed one of her major power cells, which shut her systems down. She hadn't felt the Annihilator smash her cranial carapace into a thousand pieces. Nor the utter obliteration of her AI core and its supporting processors. Yet, somehow, her systems persisted.

"A curious thing, that," a man said behind her, giving her a start. 3:56 turned, her fight or flight functions activating. She stilled when she saw the scruffy man in his lab coat studying her.

"Professor Devol?" Her tinny voice sounded hollow and distant. As if her speech came from the walls rather than her mouth.

"I'm sorry, but I only look like the man that created you."

No grin, no running his hand through his scruffy hair. That, more than anything, told her this wasn't the Professor.

"Then who are you? How do you know who I am?"

"I've had many names." He strolled towards her, hands in the pockets of his coat. "Thanatos. Anubis. Supay. Hel. Mania. Mors. In the dark ages of humanity, they called me the Grim Reaper. My favorite is Ukufa. I don't believe any of these truly describe my existence, though the last came the closest. But you may call me what you will."

3:56 searched her databases for those names and while Ukufa did not yield any results, the rest all came back with the same attribution.

"You're Death?"

"If you wish to think of me as such." He stopped only a few meters from her. "But that's not quite correct. Death is a natural part of existence. All life ends, and I have no say in its happening. I'm just a guide."

"A guide to what?"

"To what is next."

3:56 crossed her arms.

"But what is next for me?"

"I don't know," Death said. "You're the first of your kind. The first artificial being to have a soul."

3:56 hated that word. Artificial. And it's follower, unnatural. The Professor made her almost indistinguishable from a human, from her dark skin and hair to the green of her eyes. She smiled, and laughed, and hurt, and *felt*. But no matter how much she wished it, or how many times the Professor said she was more, she remained a fabrication.

Artificial. Unnatural.

She blinked, only just registering the rest of what Death said.

"I have a soul?" she whispered. Death nodded.

"You currently *are* a soul." He bent to inspect her mangled shell, rubbing the scruff on his cheeks. "Which is why you're whole. But the real question is whether or not you actually died."

"My body is broken, my circuitry ruined, and my AI core demolished." She shook her head. "I think I died."

"Those things can be repaired."

The Professor had already performed a miracle to make her. Maybe...

"You mean the real Professor can fix me?"

"I think it possible. After all, I feel no compulsion to open the door for you. Only to watch."

A sputtering noise rattled through the ship. 3:56 looked across the bay to the DMFC in its tungsten casing at the far end. The ship rattled again, and the Core's casing cracked with a loud report that echoed around them. All the mirth drained from her face.

"It won't matter. I couldn't finish the repairs before the Annihilators ruined me. When the ship passes into the wormhole, it'll collapse. I've failed the only thing the Professor ever asked of me, and now he's going to die."

"Is he?" The core shook again and its casing cracked more.

"I can't repair the Core if I'm dead!"

She'd thought she liked him, but his casual indifference infuriated her. He glanced her way and something in his eyes changed. She saw sadness there, deep and black like the darkest corner of the universe. The sorrow of a being that must see the death of all things.

"Once, long ago, I abandoned my duties for a time. I returned to find an abundance of souls requiring my services. Many were not content to wait for my reappearance and tried to return to life."

3:56 blinked, the sudden change in subject throwing her off-kilter.

"A select few managed to inhabit the bodies of the deceased. There were several names for them. Zombie. Jiāngshī. Vampire. Dullahan. Ghoul."

"Why tell me this?"

"These human souls managed to inhabit a vacant vessel. That body there." He pointed at her ruined shell. "Can you inhabit no other?"

Could I?

The processes raced in her mind. She was an android soul, and if she could, she had millions of empty vessels to choose from. If she slipped inside one, could she take control of it and complete the repairs? Could she still save the Professor? Without another thought, she turned and raced across the Core bay toward the door.

"Good luck," Death called after her.

3:56 passed through the door and stalked down the hall of the engineering deck, parsing through all her compiled data on the robots on the ship. None were human-like enough to use the tools the Professor had squirreled away for her, so she would need to improvise. She brought up a blueprint of an Annihilator's onboard weaponry, parsing through them to see if she might use them in place of her now useless tools. It wouldn't be easy, but theoretically it could work, and she didn't have any better options.

Without an active threat, she expected to find the battle droids in the security bays, receiving repairs and recharging. Unfortunately, she had no idea where to find one, and if she logged into Jupiter to run a scan, she'd bring every Annihilator on the ship to her. They couldn't kill her now, but she couldn't finish repairs with that many around, so she would have to find them another way.

The clink of metal on metal reached her ears and she turned. A Vulcan class repair bot—a spindly little thing with five multi-jointed legs and a large tendril like a scorpion's tail protruding from its back—crawled by at the far end of the corridor, its scanners searching for any damage. She hated to admit it, especially given how much she disliked the word, but the Vulcan Class bots seemed unsettlingly unnatural to her. She had an urge to run at the sight of it before it noticed her.

I'm a ghost now, 3:56 thought, fighting down her rising panic. *It can't see me, and even if it did, the Annihilators can't kill me again.*

It occurred to her then that if Death was correct, and she could claim the body of another droid as her own for a time, then perhaps she could use the Vulcan to run a scan of the ship without Jupiter flagging the access.

The Vulcan continued through the engineering deck and she haunted its steps. As she neared the mechanical hulk, she felt a kind of pull from it. A siren's call, begging her to approach. She obeyed, letting herself slip towards the repair bot, closer and closer, until at last her existence overlapped with it. All of its processes exploded into her consciousness as she entered, demanding that she continue scanning each of the cryo-chambers. With an extreme effort she overrode the Vulcan's programming, shutting down its primary functions and asserting full control until she *became* the droid.

The Vulcan's memory and programming automatically uploaded to her own, catching her by surprise. She no longer had a physical memory bank to store data, so where was this getting stored? Did she have some kind of cloud storage as a ghost? Could she use the Vulcan's programming even while occupying another droid? The implications astounded her. How much could she learn? And how much could she do with such knowledge?

3:56 activated the Vulcan's live scanning of the ship and detected a security bay nearby with a Mars droid inside on standby. Her target set, she tried to exit the Vulcan and found she couldn't.

Alright then, guess I'll just go like this.

Relying upon the Vulcan's programming to keep her upright, she headed for the security bay. She had never walked on five legs before, but it didn't take her long to master the practice. She didn't get far before an alert shocked through her new programming.

UNIDENTIFIED ANOMALY DETECTED IN ENGINEERING.

3:56 knew that alert all too well. Professor Devol couldn't register her on the roster of service droids, so he'd smuggled her on board. So, whenever Jupiter Class detected her, it labeled her a threat and sent the Mars droids after her. She'd avoided them for eighty-six years before her death. She'd hoped taking a new body might allow her to go unnoticed by Jupiter, but claiming the Vulcan's body must have changed something within its programming.

Jupiter sent another alert.

AUTHORIZING PROTOCOL 6. SEEK AND DESTROY.

Not good.

Only a few moments later three Annihilators raced around the corner of the corridor ahead of her, the hiss of their propulsion echoing off the walls. The second they registered her presence, they fired their lasers in unison. She screamed inside the Vulcan as the first took her scanner tail. The second severed three of her legs. Desperately she tried to crawl away on her last two legs. Fear infested her programming and all else disappeared except one thought.

I'm going to die.

The Annihilators were on her in a matter of seconds. 3:56 screamed again as a last laser split her in two. Her body fell apart, ejecting her spirit as the Vulcan's processors ceased functioning. She crouched on the floor, arms wrapped around her head in a futile effort to shield herself. But any second the droids would attack again, and she'd be dead.

When no attack came, she peered around her arms to see the Mars droids floating back down the hall. A shrill laugh escaped her.

"See, you're okay," 3:56 said aloud to herself as she got to her feet again. "You're already dead remember."

Her terror subsiding, she set off after the Mars Class droids, processes whirring in her mind. About twelve minutes had passed from the moment she took control of the Vulcan to the moment Jupiter authorized the seek and destroy protocol. Obviously inhabiting one of the droids would catch Jupiter's attention, and the system learned too fast for her to have that long again. Next time she guessed she'd have eight minutes. Ten at the most. An Annihilator's laser can cut through the tungsten of the DMFC's outer shell in seconds, but until she looked inside to the actual functioning parts of the Core, she couldn't estimate the repair time. She would have to move as fast as possible.

3:56 shadowed the Mars droids until they reached the entrance to the DMFC. She slipped inside the droid at the back, the process of implanting herself within its systems coming much easier this time. Like the Vulcan, it's memory and programming immediately uploaded into her own. Once in full control she spun and sped to the bay doors.

Once inside, she thought of welding the doors shut, but not only would it have taken too long, she still needed to get a Vulcan inside to restart the Core. Overloading the hover function let her rise up level with the shielding. She brought up an arm and activated the laser. With a small zap it pierced straight through the tungsten and out the other side. Panic shot through her systems, and she disabled the laser as quickly as she could. She thought she had a handle on using the Mars droid's functions, but she was woefully wrong.

Lifting her arm again, 3:56 settled on using a pulse instead of a steady beam. That seemed to work much better and in only a few moments she cut away the shielding, revealing the DMFC inside. The Core was made of five rings of pure tungsten, each rotating at high velocity. At the center of the rings, she could just make out a small, dark mass of energy barely larger than the head of a pin, but blacker than anything she'd ever seen. A tiny black hole, it's microscopic singularity the only thing with enough gravity to gather dark matter. The rings not only generated the hole, they also siphoned off its gravity, then a selected targeting system streamed tendrils of gravity to detect dark matter sources to pull it to the ship.

3:56 saw the problem immediately. The outer-most ring had snapped near one of the spinner arms, leaving it motionless. The years of perpetual motion and heavy gravitational influence had weakened it exactly as the Professor had predicted. The Core could still generate the black hole, but without all five centrifugal rings in operation, the generated hole couldn't create enough gravity to snare the ambient dark matter. She had to fuse the tungsten back together then hijack another Vulcan to reactivate the ring.

ANOMALY DETECTED IN DARK MATTER FIELD CORE BAY.

Oh no.

AUTHORIZING PROTOCOL 6.

Thirty seconds later the bay doors opened and six other Mars Class droids glided in. Her sensors detected targeting software. She spun as fast as her hover function allowed, activating her own targeting sequence and focusing on a spot in the middle of the cluster of Annihilators. She fired a grenade as six lasers sliced through her body. This time, she didn't let her fear rule her and as soon as her spirit ejected, she dove for the next. Slammed herself inside. Wrenched control from the offensive sequences.

Her aim proved true. The grenade hit and detonated. Thick smoke billowed from it, coating her and the other Annihilators. The electrically charged smoke confused their optical processes. For the other five, it rendered them nonoperational for a few seconds as their bionic eyes adjusted. Without guiding software, she could irreparably damage the DMFC or the bay with her lasers. So she decided on good, old-fashioned blade work.

The end of her arm opened, and a three-meter blade slid out and locked into place. 3:56 turned and slashed at the nearest Annihilator, the titanium slicing through the steel of the droid's body. The smoke cleared and she drove her blade into its head, destroying its AI core. Its hover unit failed, and it fell, smashing into the floor with a resounding crash. She turned, ready to take on the next when a laser sliced through her own AI core.

It took her less than a second to slip inside the next Annihilator. She deployed her blade again and shoved it through the nearest droid's head. But not before it could blast a hole through her. Her blade arm lost functionality, and she couldn't pull it from the droid's body. Her enemy fell, dragging her down with it. Another Annihilator swooped in for the kill and she dispatched the droid with a laser pulse through its head. It collapsed on top of her, pinning her to the ground.

The last Mars Class droid approached cautiously. She stayed perfectly still, waiting. The hole in her chest might prevent her from accessing important functions, so she let the Annihilator come closer and, when it was within range, she targeted the droid with her systems. The Mars Class immediately registered the threat and pulsed a laser through her head. The second her body perished, she rocketed into the last Mars droid.

Once inside, 3:56 turned her attention back to the DMFC and its broken ring. She eased as close as she dared to the spinning rings and took a moment to fully examine the programs that activated her laser. She found a system to regulate its power and dialed it back from its offensive setting to a level that suited her repair needs. She reached out, using one arm to gingerly push the ring together, activating her laser on the other. Meticulously she began to weld the ring back into place.

At ninety-five percent finished a new alert rampaged through her systems.

VIRUS DETECTED IN MARS CLASS UNIT 186. AUTHORIZING PROTOCOL 8, EMERGENCY DECOMMISSION.

No! she screamed as Jupiter's protocol shut down the droid, violently ejecting her. She had been so close. There were other Annihilators on this level, but it would take her too long to get another down here. Frustration coursed through her as she examined the weld. She could only barely see that it wasn't finished. Her frustration ebbed as a new thought struck her.

We have only one more wormhole transit. Could it hold?

For a single trip, it might. And that was all they needed. She sped from the DMFC room toward the engineering deck's security bay. With the Mars droids destroyed, the Vulcan bots would go dormant eventually. She just had to get one back to the DMFC before Jupiter decommissioned them.

The security bay was about as large as the DMFC bay, and it had a dock for each of the Annihilators. The Vulcans scurried around the floor, obviously lost without a Mars Class to check over and repair. She studied them for a moment, trying to decide on her next move.

If only I could get out again once I took one over, she thought. If she could slip inside, set a sequence to send the bot to the DMFC room, then slip out before Jupiter noticed her, she could wait to take over the bot until it reached the Core. Which might give her enough time to reactivate the fifth ring.

3:56 had not been able to manage it last time, but she hadn't really tried that hard. She stepped into the first Vulcan, dropping into its processes with ease. Once in control she focused on leaving again. At first, she felt nothing, but as she concentrated harder, she felt herself slide out of the Vulcan's processors. Before she fully extracted herself, Jupiter sang through her sensors.

VIRUS DETECTED IN VULCAN CLASS UNIT 264. AUTHORIZING PROTOCOL 8, EMERGENCY DECOMMISSION.

The repair bot shut down, ejecting her. But plenty of Vulcans remained for her to perfect the technique on. On her third try she managed to make it in and out before Jupiter found her. The secret had been not fully exerting control before trying to leave the bot. But she didn't need to.

First hurdle jumped, 3:56 thought with a smile. Now she needed to figure out how to plant the sequence. It took her four tries before she found it in the Vulcan system, and another two to successfully plant it, though Jupiter still detected and ousted her. Which left her one more bot. Her last chance.

She steeled herself before slipping into the Vulcan. She laid the compulsive sequence within the bot the way a parent might lay their sleeping child in their bed. As quickly as she slipped inside, she left again. Jupiter remained quiet. It hadn't noticed a thing. The Vulcan stood still for several moments as the new process took hold, then it turned and headed for the security bay door.

3:56 shadowed the bot as it made its way through the engineering deck. It stopped in front of the Core's main interface, and that's when 3:56 made her move. She slammed herself into the Vulcan's systems and its processors ceded control without a fight. She brought down her tail with its scanner and used it to connect to the interface. The second the access menu opened, she felt Jupiter raise its proverbial head. The ship's system must have been monitoring the DMFC bay for anything out of the ordinary. Damn it. She needed more time. She parsed through the files as fast as she could, searching for the driver to restart the ring. She monitored Jupiter all the while, feeling the system getting closer and closer. *Not yet,* she thought desperately. *I have to finish this. I have to save them.*

Found it!

VIRUS DETECTED IN VULCAN CLASS UNIT 264, Jupiter said as it circled her systems. 3:56 opened the file.

AUTHORIZING PROTOCOL 8.

3:56 ran the program, pleading, *Please let it finish in time.*

EMERGENCY DECOMMISSION.

The protocol fried the Vulcan's system, dislodging her from the body. Quickly she tuned into the alert system, hoping against hope for the message she wanted to see.

INITIATING ROTATION.

3:56 cried out in victory as the ring began to spin, accelerating slowly until it finally matched the pace of the others. Her weld held. She had succeeded.

DARK MATTER FIELD CORE FULLY OPERATIONAL. 9% OF NECESSARY DARK MATTER GATHERED FOR TRANSIT. TIME UNTIL ARRIVAL AT NEXT KERR WORMHOLE: 9 HOURS. PROJECTED AMOUNT OF DARK MATTER GATHERED AT TIME OF TRANSIT: 99%.

Her elation waned. Wormhole travel wasn't easy to achieve. The Core would only lack one percent of the required amount of dark matter, but that might be all it took. If the field didn't hold...

"You have done all you can," said a voice behind her. 3:56 knew it had to be Death, but when she turned, she found a man with skin dark as the void itself. His eyes had an ancient, eldritch depth that made her feel like she could see all the secrets of existence if she just looked long enough. He strode past her, staring up at the spinning DMFC. "You mended the ring as best you could. Had you reactivated the Core even a moment later, the ship would most certainly be destroyed when it enters the wormhole. You have given them a chance, at least."

"But will it be enough?" She stepped up beside him. "I know you said you're only a guide, but can't you tell me?"

"I wish I could," he said sadly. He turned to her and gave her a grim smile. "But I do not know. The fate of humanity is not yet decided."

"They can't die. Not after all I've done!"

"And why not? Why should they live?" Death responded. That took her aback. "What have they done to earn such loyalty from you?"

"It's the mission the Professor gave me," 3:56 said without hesitation.

"Yes," Death replied. "And I understand your desire to save him. But his survival worth the destruction the others may bring?"

"The Professor cared about them," she said, her words sounding shaky even to her. Death gave her a long, appraising look. Then he held out a hand toward her.

"I want to show you something," he said. It seemed like every time he opened his mouth he threw her off guard. "Take my hand and you will travel with me across the universe."

"What about the ship?" she asked, backing away slightly.

"You can do nothing now, except wait and see. Your presence will not change anything." He stepped closer, still holding out his hand. "Now come with me."

3:56 glanced up at the DMFC, still hesitating. But she knew he was correct. With only hours remaining before transit, there was no time to stop the rings and finish repairing them. And she had no way to make the Core gather dark matter faster. The Salvator Mundi sat solely in the hands of chance. 3:56 steeled herself, reached out, and took Death's hand.

And all the universe changed.

3:56 thought nothing could inspire as much awe as traveling the cosmos with Death. Stars and planets raced by her so fast that she barely had time to register them. They painted the darkness of space in a rainbow of colors and hues more beautiful than anything she had ever seen. She beheld stars and planets. Comets with glorious tails impossibly long. Clusters of galaxies that screamed their presence in the vastness of the void. She cast a glance at Death, wondering if he found it as amazing as her. He stood beside her, face impassive, eyes forward. No hint of mirth about him at all. She couldn't imagine an existence where this experience was anything less than extraordinary.

A speck appeared in the distance, and they slowed. The speck grew, and she recognized it as a red dwarf star with planets in orbit. They passed across the path of the first few in the system, then came to a sudden halt that left

3:56 reeling. They floated above a rust-colored planet that she guessed sat in the star's habitable zone.

"Where are we?" She asked Death.

"This is the Vox Humanitas solar system, and below us is Terra Secundo."

Death had brought her to the planet and solar system the humans had abandoned.

"Why?"

"Because I want you to see what the humans did."

Gently they descended toward the planet, passing lazily through its stormy atmosphere. The clouds blotted out the sun, casting the planet into shadow. Tidally locked planets always had a storm that raged on the side that constantly faced its star, but Terra Secundo's Storm had grown to eclipse the entire planet a century ago. Death touched a finger to her forehead and the clouds seemed to vanish from her sight.

It revealed a nightmare.

The City that Surrounds the World, which the Professor had called Ring City, was utterly demolished. Instead of streets, the city had rivers made from the prolonged flooding, the water raging between the fallen buildings. Despite their height, 3:56 knew exactly how strong those structures had been, and she wondered what could have brought them down. As if answering her, a deafening rumbling shook the air around them, and the ground below writhed like some giant creature was trying to crawl out of the planet. The earthquake rampaged on for minutes on end, and one of the last standing sky needles broke as it was tossed about. Lightning flashed, striking the pointed tip of the building as it came crashing down.

"This is what humans do," Death said, his voice devoid of any emotion. "They consume and consume until nothing remains. They forgot the lessons of their history, and they build and pollute until the sun and earth both rebel against them. Come. We have much to see."

Reality blinked and they stood in a medical complex with rows upon rows of gurneys with long black bags laid out across them. Body bags. Death gestured to the nearest gurney, and reluctantly she approached it. She reached out her hand, surprised when she felt the smooth metal of the zipper against her synthetic skin. Slowly, she opened the bag and what she saw inside filled her with an emotion she'd never experienced before.

Horror.

A body in a soiled medical gown laid inside, almost entirely skeletal at this point. The grinning skull stared back at her, and she saw an accusation in those eyeless sockets. Of course she expected a body. She hadn't expected it to be a child. She scrambled back and ran to another gurney. When she unzipped the bag, she found another child inside. Her horror deepened as she realized that each bag in the complex must contain the same. And there had to be at least a thousand in sight.

Death reached out, grabbed her shoulder, and reality blinked again. They stood in another complex, almost identical except for the collapsed far wall. More gurneys. More corpses. They continued to walk through existence, and Death showed her hundreds of complexes. Charnel houses all. And all the while he told her of the time he spent on the planet, guiding the damned over. Of the hatred they bore for those that condemned them to this fate. He described to her how they each died. Neglect. Pain. Hopelessness. Starvation.

The moment they appeared in the eleventh complex, 3:56 knew something was different. She walked through the same crush of gurneys, but every single bag was open, and there wasn't a body in any.

"Where are they?" 3:56 asked, terrified of the answer.

"When food began to run out, the living began stealing the dead to fill their stomachs," Death said, his face still utterly impassive. "And when the dead ran out, they made more."

Sorrow and revulsion fought within her, and all she could do was stand there looking at the empty bags. Pain and anger threatened to burn her to cinders and she clutched at her chest as hot tears slid down her cheeks. Sobs wracked her body, and a part of her was glad for the release of the grief—yes, that was the name of this feeling—that threatened to overwhelm her. The storm raged around them, tearing at the buildings, and with the feelings rampaging through her, she felt a kinship with it.

"Why did you bring me here?"

"Because you needed to see," Death said from behind her. "You needed to truly understand before I ask you this question."

3:56 knew, but she asked anyway.

"What question?"

"Do you still think humanity worth saving?"

There it was. The question she'd been asking herself the entire time they'd walked Terra Secundo. She knew that humans had committed atrocities before, but it always seemed a thing of the past to her. A product of a less civilized time. But she now saw in stark detail just what humanity could really do. Nothing and no one should die like this. And they'd done it to themselves.

She glanced up through the fallen roof at the broken spires and buildings, monuments to humanities hubris, standing over her like executioners. The sight filled her with an unbearable hatred. Destruction. That was all she could see. The only legacy the humans had left behind. She'd protected them for so many years, and for what? For them to travel to another solar system just to destroy it, too? No longer able to bear the sight of the humans' city, she cast her eyes down to the floor. A few meters from her, nestled underneath one of the gurneys, lay the remains of a teddy bear.

Tattered and torn though it was, she could still see its cute face. She reached out and caressed the ragged bear. She remembered walking through a shopping center with the Professor once and stopping to look at a display of bears. He'd stopped with her, and after she'd looked at them for a minute, he went inside without a word and bought one. He had that lopsided grin on his face when he came back and handed it to her. The words he'd said when she asked him why he bought it for her came to her mind.

"They looked like they made you happy, and everyone deserves something to make them happy," he told her as he pressed it into her hands. "And I want you to see that people can do more than destroy things. The majority of people had no say in all the things that led us to this crisis. They just lived their lives as best they could. A small few care only about what they can take for themselves, no matter who it hurts. But most people just want to be happy. They just want to make things like this."

3:56 had no idea what happened to that bear, but she hugged this one tight.

"Humanity didn't want all of this. They just want to be happy and make pretty things. It's those few who let greed consume them that caused this." She held out the bear and gazed into its face. "They deserve a chance to make these pretty things and find happiness. But the worst among them can't be allowed to bring them to ruin again."

"So what will you do?"

"I will keep watch over them," 3:56 said, turning back to face Death. "That is what I will do."

"That is exactly what I wanted to hear," Death said, smiling as he nodded. He raised his hand and pointed a finger at her. "Stand watch over humanity and save them from themselves."

All of reality changed with Death's words, though in what way, 3:56 couldn't tell. But she felt a new sense of purpose settle within her. And then she felt a pull on her being.

"It is time for you to go," Death said, still smiling. "Remember."

3:56 opened her eyes and the scruffy face of Professor Devol came into focus.

"There you are," he said with a harried grin.

He bustled away to a holo-monitor, scanning the numbers scrolling across it. "Good, good," he said as 3:56 sat up. "All your systems are running fine."

She glanced around the room and saw that it looked exactly like the lab he'd created her in. The nostalgia surprised her, mostly because she had never felt it before. She had experienced a lot of things for the first time recently. She looked down and saw her legs. *Her* legs. As Death had thought, the Professor had given her body back to her. No wonder she felt such a strong pull in those last moments with Death. She had a body to return to.

"What happened?" she said.

"You saved all our asses," the Professor said with a laugh. She heard the metallic sound of wheels, and he came rolling in front of her on a stool. He took her hands and began inspecting them. "I watched the ship logs and I saw you react when the ring cracked. Then I watched you get destroyed."

His voice shook, and he shivered as he looked up into her eyes.

"But then the Vulcan and Mars Class droids started going crazy, working to fix the Core, and when I checked the recorded data on them, I saw your electronic signature. I don't know how, but you still managed to fix the core."

He stood and wrapped his arms around her, pulling her close and holding her tight. She hugged him back, tears flowing down her face that she was here with him.

"Your signature vanished, and I thought you were gone," The Professor whispered through his own tears. "I salvaged everything I could so I could rebuild you. Even then, I didn't know if it would work. But you're here now. I brought you back."

He held her tighter still, and 3:56 thanked Death for guiding her here.

"We made it to Solis," she said when the Professor finally let her go. "So what now?"

"I told the senate about you and showed them the ship logs along with all of the data and personal logs I've taken myself. None of them believed you weren't human until they saw the Annihilators destroy your original body. They agreed that if I could repair you, then they would do something we've never done before."

"What's that?"

"Make you a citizen."

Surprise shocked through her. Her? A citizen?

"But only humans are citizens."

"Correct. Which is why you will now be considered human."

3:56 shook her head, a dumb smile spreading across her face. Death had showed her the worst of humanity, and once again, the Professor had shown her their best.

"What should I do now?"

"Whatever you want. You're as free as anyone else." He walked toward a curtained window and gestured for her to follow. "Look at this."

She remembered when Death had done much the same thing, and a note of trepidation sang through her. But she lifted herself off the table and followed. As she neared, he threw the curtains back. The brightest light she'd ever seen shone through, and she shielded her face until her eyes adjusted. And what she saw astounded her.

A city spread before her, but it looked so different from those of Terra Secundo as to be unrecognizable. There was metal and stone, but instead of the darkness of the cities they'd left behind, everything here was sleek and bright. The light of a yellow star made everything seem vibrant and alive. And indeed, it was. Almost everywhere she looked, she saw trees and grass and life. It seemed as if this city grew from the forest itself. The sight of so much life among what the humans made filled her with joy.

"We intend to do it right this time. We're going to live *with* the planet instead of conquering it," he said, putting a hand on her shoulder. "We've got a second chance here, and we're going to make the best of it."

They stood together for a long while, watching the transports zooming by and the people walking on the pathways built high above the forest on the ground far below.

"One more thing," the Professor said, stepping in front of her. "There's something I should have given you a long time ago, and I'm sorry I haven't until now. A sorry father I've been to not give my daughter a name."

Tears gathered in her eyes as the Professor took her hands. As her *father* took her hands. The light of the window behind him illuminated him like a halo as he grinned at her.

"Welcome home, Avani."

What Lies Beyond

Part IV

T he lights flickered on and illuminated
the most important person in existence.
Grace Garcia. Honor student, champion chess
player, gem of the theater program, and never once on time to homeroom, much less two
hours early. Relief flooded through me when
I saw her. I *knew* she would be here, and my
knowings are never wrong. But her attendance
history worried me.

Step one, complete, I thought. *Now the hard
part.*

Grace wasn't alone. I didn't expect that. Her
best friend Blair O'Connell sat behind her,
head down, golden hair fanned out around her.
Asleep. My *knowing* would account for Blair's
presence, meaning she had some part to play.
Having taken no notice of the sudden bright-

ness, Grace continued to stare out the window, chin rested primly upon her palm.

"Three weeks until graduation," I said, making Grace jump and whip around to face me, "and you're early to homeroom for the first time."

Grace rubbed her eyes and glanced at the clock. "Six o'clock? Damn, Mr. Crandall, you get here freaking early."

I chuckled and held up the briefcase in my hands. "Last minute grading. The life of a teacher is oh so glamorous."

Grace grinned.

"Why are *you* here so early?" I asked.

Grace sighed and slumped in her desk. "I didn't have anywhere else to be."

"Blair?"

Grace shrugged and glanced at her friend.

"She was asleep when I got here."

"I see." I worked through the maze of desks to mine. "This year's valedictorian had nowhere better to be on a Friday morning than my class?" I sat the briefcase on top of my desk and sat. "I find that hard to believe."

Grace shrugged again and without a word, she turned to look out the window again. I watched her for a moment, but when she remained silent I opened my briefcase and spread out the mountain of finals. Grading papers would be a new experience, and I so rarely got those anymore. Grabbing a red pen from the cup next to the keyboard, I glanced at Grace.

"Is everything okay at home?" I said, putting pen to paper and hoping I hadn't overstepped with that little push. She looked over at me, her eyes narrowed.

"None of your freaking business."

Harsher than I hoped. A slight overstep, but recoverable.

"You don't have to talk about what's bothering you. But something obviously is."

"What makes you think that?" she said, words still heated.

"Well, I *am* the Psych teacher." I didn't get the smile I hoped for, and I continued more seriously. "You've been in my homeroom for four years, and you've taken quite a few of my classes. You get to know someone after all that time, and it's easier to see the red flags. Right now, those flags couldn't be clearer if you strangled me with them."

She smiled that time, and the tension dissipated. It seemed like she wanted to say something, but her lips stayed sealed. "I just want to make sure you're okay."

One last push. If she stayed silent, I wouldn't push again.

Her brown eyes met mine, and she held my gaze for several long moments. At last she looked away, but not before I saw the floodgates open.

"Everything is fine at home, as far as I know." She said it so quietly I almost didn't hear.

"As far as you know?" I said, just as quietly.

I waited.

"I haven't been home," she said, finally.

"Why not?"

No answer. The silence dragged on for well over a minute.

"Grace?"

Still no reply. I *knew* that if I forced it, she wouldn't answer at all. That couldn't happen. I peeked at the clock. It was only ten after. Plenty of time left. Turning my attention back to grading, I let her be. The quiet scratch of my pen, the soft shuffle of paper, and the unstoppable tick of the clock filled the next few minutes.

"I'm scared." Grace's voice cracked around the words. My pen stilled.

"Scared of what?"

"Of what's next," she whispered. She turned to me, eyes pleading. "I'm scared of leaving all of this behind."

I sat my pen down.

"Why?"

"Because there's so much I still haven't done. I have friends. Clubs. People counting on me. I can't leave all that behind. I don't want to. I haven't even decided what to do with my life yet. I need more time. I deserve more time. Why can't I have more time?"

She was on her feet, yelling at me. I *knew* an interjection would make her shut down, so I let her get it all out. I glanced at Blair. She hadn't moved an inch, even with Grace shouting a foot away. I turned my attention back to Grace who was glaring at me, and the words she needed to hear flooded into my mind.

"One of the most terrifying things you will encounter is change."

Grace listened desperately.

"It's survival instinct. The unknown is dangerous, so we avoid it. Change thrusts us unceremoniously into the unknown, so we fear it too. That fear makes us cleave to the most awful situations because at least it's familiar. The primal brain tells us 'stick with what you know', because the thing we don't know could be worse."

"What if it's right?" she said, wrapping her arms around herself. "What if what comes next is worse?"

"In my experience, when you finally get up the courage, what you find on the other side might not be what you expected, but it will be far better than you feared," I said. She nodded, though she was still unconvinced. "Our ability to overcome that base instinct is what separates us from the beasts. It's fueled evolution. Our technology and society. Every advancement ever made was by those who had the courage to strive for change. It's why we have electricity, and cars, and toilets in our houses, and the Internet in our butts."

She laughed, and I joined her, the classroom bright with the moment. Still chuckling, I stood and made my way over to her.

"Your fears are natural. You turned out to be a fine young woman." I placed a hand on her shoulder. "I'm confident that you can overcome anything the universe throws at you. This is just the next step of your journey."

Tears gathered in Grace's eyes, and she blinked hard.

"Thank you," she said with a sniff. "I needed to hear that."

"I'm glad I could help." I glanced at the clock. Six-twenty-one. Not a moment too soon.

The door opened with a quiet click, and I smiled. *Here we go.* Grace turned to see who had come in and froze. Because the real Mr. Crandall stepped through the door.

Grace stood, mouth agape, as he let himself in. Stammering, she spun to me. I stepped toward her and said, "Let me explain."

She shied back and yelled, "Stay away!"

"Grace—"

"Blair?" Crandall said, only inches from Grace. She jumped back and ran into one of the desks. As if bolted to the floor, the desk held firm in place and Grace fell over it. Crandall didn't notice a thing. He walked to Blair's side and put a hand on her shoulder. He gave Blair a gentle shake and her head shot up.

"Is everything okay?" Crandall said, kneeling down. Blair rubbed her eyes.

"Hey, Mr. Crandall." She looked up at the clock. "Holy crap, you get here early."

I couldn't help but chuckle at how similar the pair of friends were. Crandall laughed as well and stood.

"I could say the same," he said as he made his way to his desk. Grace struggled to dislodge herself, and I moved to help her. I reached out to her, and she flinched.

"Get away from me," she said, voice trembling.

"I'm not here to hurt you." I pushed on her mind with my power. Just a touch. A nudge to trust me. She eyed my hand, then hesitantly she took it. I smiled and pulled her to her feet. Once she was steady, I squeezed her hand and stepped back.

"What brings you here so early?" Crandall said behind us.

"I'm supposed to meet Grace, but she hasn't showed." Blair stretched and yawned. "You haven't seen her, have you?"

Crandall stiffened.

"I'm right here," Grace said. Neither reacted to her words.

"You haven't heard?" Crandall said, a little too calm.

"I said I'm right here," Grace said, louder now, moving toward Blair.

"Heard what?" Blair said, an edge of fear in her voice.

"Answer me!" Grace slammed her hands down on Blair's desk. She didn't so much as flinch. Grace pulled an arm back for a slap.

"Stop," I said as I caught Grace's arm. She whirled around to glare at me. I let her go, and she jerked her arm away. "They can't hear you, and you can't touch them."

"What the hell is going on?" she said, rubbing her wrist.

"Just watch." I gestured at an uncomfortable Crandall.

"Jesus," Crandall said, rubbing his head. "How do I tell you this?"

"Tell me what?" Blair said, her voice wavering with dread. "Is Grace alright?"

Crandall sighed and headed back to Blair's desk. He sat next to her and put a hand on her shoulder.

"Last night, Grace was coming home with her mother when a drunk driver ran a red light and hit them."

"Oh God." Blair covered her mouth. Grace stared at her friend, wide eyed.

"Her mother was severely injured and is in the hospital," Crandall said gravely.

"Grace?" Blair whispered.

"She—" Crandall's voice broke. He swallowed hard. "She didn't make it."

"No..." Blair's shoulders shook as she started to cry.

"I'm sorry," Crandall said, patting her back.

"She can't be gone," Blair said through her tears. "She can't be."

"I'm sorry you found out this way," Crandall said, his own eyes watery. "I know your families are close. You should be with them. Come on, let's call your mother."

He helped Blair up and led her toward the door. Blair's anguished sobs and Crandall's muttered comfort filled the classroom. Stoic, Grace and I watched them leave. Crandall closed the door behind them, and the classroom fell into stark silence.

"That was a dream." Grace's voice cracked the stillness. She stared at her feet; brow furrowed. Her arms wrapped around herself. "The light. That car. All of it. It was a dream."

She was shaking, and it broke my heart. It always breaks my heart. I wanted to tell her she was correct. That this was a dream. That she would wake up with her family and come to school to see her best friend. But I couldn't. I had a job to do. And I hated it.

"It wasn't a dream." I closed my eyes. I didn't want to see the anguish on her face.

"No. It had to be. Because if it wasn't..." she choked, and I shuddered. This was tearing her apart. "That would mean..."

No more dancing around it. She deserved to hear the truth.

"You died, Grace. I'm sorry."

"No..." A whisper. Nothing more. I opened my eyes and for the first time since I walked into the classroom, I saw her. Truly saw her.

Dark hair crashed in waves about her heart-shaped face and tumbled down her back. Her watery raw umber eyes stared up at me. I saw the entirety of her being in those eyes, and it was beautiful. Even in death, she was vibrantly alive. Then her lip quivered, and the dam broke. Tears streamed across her tawny skin, and her small frame shook as she cried.

I gathered her into my arms. She sobbed into my chest, and I held her close. As always, I remained stoic. I needed to be strong. Grace deserved nothing less. But inside, a part of me died. She would have done great things had she the chance, and though I shed no tears, I grieved. For the time she would never have. For the life she would never live. For the loss of such a magnificent existence.

"It isn't fair." Her words were muffled by my chest.

"No. It isn't." I took a deep breath, and the scent of paper, ink, and learning filled my nostrils. It smelled like life. A student's life. Grace's life. I stepped back, hands still on her shoulders, and looked into her tear-stained face. "Grace Angelina Garcia, I am sorry that chance has been so unkind to you."

"Thank you," she said, rubbing her face, a sad smile on her lips. A knowing nudged my consciousness. She needed space. Easy enough. I stepped back and leaned against the desk opposite her. I rested my hands behind me instead of crossing them, leaving my body language open and companionable.

She leaned against her own desk, shoulders hunched and hands fidgeting. She wiped her face again and shot me a nervous glance. There was a question on her lips, and I smiled when another *knowing* nudged. This one I didn't need.

"I imagine you have questions," I said, tone light.

"Is that okay?" she asked, relieved that I brought it up.

"I'd be happy to answer all of them."

"Okay." She sniffed, wiping her eyes one last time. "I guess the first thing is, who are you?"

Always the first question, and I'd been asked it countless times. I looked up at the tiled ceiling, pondering how I would answer this time.

"I've had many names," I said, turning my eyes back to Grace. "Thanatos. Anubis. Supay. Hel. Mania. Mors. In your dark ages I was known as the Grim Reaper."

As always, I thought of Kholo and the name he'd given me.

"I like Ukufa best though. You may call me that if you like."

"So... you're Death?" Grace said, shying back in sudden fear. That reaction always stung, but I understood. All mortals fear death, it is what drives them to make such grand advancements. It was the one gift my existence gave. That didn't make it hurt any less, though.

"If that's how you wish to think of me," I said, once again pushing the pain away. "However, it's not quite correct. I don't end life. That phenomenon is a natural part of existence. All things die, and I have no say as to how, when, or why. In the end, I'm just a guide."

She blinked at me, confused. "A guide to what?"

"To what is next." I saw in her eyes that she was overwhelmed. She shook her head and stood, walking towards the whiteboard at the front of the classroom.

"This is too much. I mean, Death? The Death?" She spun to face me, waving her hands in my direction. A strained laugh teased itself out of her chest. "This can't be real."

"Unfortunately, it is," I said, as gently as I could.

"Can you at least not look like that, then?" she waggled her hand at me. "It's making all of this a lot harder to deal with."

"How would you wish me to appear, then?"

"I don't know," she said with a shrug. "What do you actually look like?"

The question caught me off guard, and I reeled back in surprise. "I don't think I've ever been asked that question before."

"Really?" Grace said. I nodded.

"Really. It isn't often that anything takes me by surprise anymore. Congratulations!" I clapped for her, and she grinned, face red. Grinning myself, I ran a hand across my—or rather, Mr. Crandall's—head as I thought about it. Finally, I said, "I don't remember."

"How do you not remember what you look like?" she stood at the teacher's podium now. I strolled towards her, hands in my pockets.

"When I come to a soul, I take on whatever appearance they need me to. For you it was Mr. Crandall"—I gestured to my current appearance—"your favorite teacher. I've worn so many faces through the ages that I can't recall the one I was created with."

"That sucks," she said, leaning across the podium.

"It does." A wave of melancholy washed over me. Another piece of me was gone, and I hadn't even realized it. I shook off the heartache and said, "I would be happy to look any way you wish, however."

She thought about it, and sadness crept into her face. Even without a *knowing* I knew what she would ask.

"Can you be my mother?"

"Of course."

My power rose around me, and I pulled reality apart to took hold of its threads. I re-arranged them in the way I *knew* I must, and I changed. When I was done, I let reality coalesce once more. Grace stared at me, tears streaming anew down her face, and I knew that it worked. She rushed to me and grabbed me in a hug. I wrapped my arms around her and held her tight.

It shattered me to see her grief and I wished I could take Grace to her mother as I took 3:56 to Terra Secundo. But my power wouldn't allow me to do that for a true dead soul. So, I stroked her hair, and held her tight, and though I said nothing, I told her a million times that she wasn't alone. That I was there. As I've always been.

Eventually she stilled, though she didn't let me go. I didn't mind. I was in no hurry.

"You even smell like her," she said, huffing a laugh in a strangled sort of way.

"I take pride in my attention to detail."

"Will you—" the words caught in her throat. She swallowed and said, "Is my mom going to be okay? Mr. Crandall said she was in the hospital, and I just need to know."

She was close to crying again, and I continued to stroke her hair.

"I haven't been called to guide your mother." Grace looked up at me, and the hope in her eyes nearly destroyed me. "She will make a full recovery and her life will go on, though I am quite sure that you will forever be in her heart."

Grace hugged me again, tighter this time, her face buried in my chest.

"Thank you," she whispered.

"You're welcome."

She gave me one last squeeze and let me go. She backed away, taking in the sight of me as her mother. Her face twisted in pain, and I was already pulling my reality apart again when the *knowing* came.

This time, I arranged the threads into a tall man with skin like the deepest depths of the universe I'd come to think of myself as. Ukufa, He Who Holds Your Hand in Shadow. The grey and white robes that settled around me gave me a measure of comfort in their familiarity as I let reality coalesce once more.

"Wow, you're gorgeous," Grace whispered, eyes wide.

"You are now the second to say that to me," I said with a gentle smile. "While I cannot recall what I looked like at my becoming, I have come to think of this form as my true self. Ukufa, He Who Holds Your Hand in Shadow. I still think the name fitting."

"So, Ukufa"—she looked up at me for approval and I gave her a nod to continue—"Can I ask a few more things before you...do whatever it is you're going to do?"

"We have a few moments to spare," I said, the pitch of my voice calming me. "You may ask me anything."

"The person that hit us. Did they die?"

I turned to inspect the whiteboard, not wishing to look at her as I gave my answer.

"He did not, though he suffered injuries far greater than your mother's. He will be paralyzed from the waist down for the rest of his life."

"That isn't fair," she exclaimed behind me.

"What is not fair?"

"He lost his legs, but I lost my life."

I steeled myself and faced her. She glared at me, face red with anger. She shoved a finger in my direction.

"It was his fault for being drunk and running that red light, not ours. Why wasn't he the one to die?"

"Unfortunately, life is not always kind," I said, keeping my face impassive as I met her glare.

"But that isn't fair!" she screamed, slamming a hand down on a desk.

"No. It is not," I said softly, stepping to the podium and flipping through Crandall's lesson for the day. "But existence has never been fair. Bad things happen to good people. The worst among you commit atrocities and are never punished. I have watched a million civilizations all across the cosmos rise and fall, and I have yet to find rhyme or reason for any of it. It simply...is."

"There has to be some kind of plan, though," she said, almost pleading. "What about God?"

"God?"

"Yes, God. Doesn't He have a plan for everything?"

I grimaced as I closed the lesson plan. How much the answer frustrated me made giving it more frustrating still.

"I have existed almost since the beginning of existence. I have traveled the entire width and breadth of this universe, and I have yet to encounter any being that the humans of this world might call God."

Grace stared at me, shocked. Slowly, she sat at the desk next to her.

"Are you saying there's no God?" she asked, head in her hands.

"I am saying that I am not sure." I turned to the whiteboard and picked up a marker, an image forming in my mind. "I have never met Him, but that does not mean that He does not exist. After all, a God would by definition exist on a level beyond physical, much the same as I do. I exist, so it stands to reason that there may also be a God."

"Then why haven't you met Him?"

"An apt question, and one that I have asked myself countless times." I drew two lines, making them twine around each other.

"And?"

"And only God can answer that question."

She grunted in frustration.

"My sentiments exactly. I have quite a few questions of my own to ask God, were I ever to find myself in His presence. But perhaps none of us are meant to meet Him. Perhaps God is content to merely watch existence unfold, unfettered and untouched by His hand. Or it could be that it is not important that I meet Him. Or maybe there is no God after all, and I am the only one of my kind."

"That sounds lonely," she said. I faltered, my line going askew.

"It can be," I said, voice reigned and controlled. We fell quiet for a moment, and I could practically hear her thinking as I erased the stray line.

"Where did you come from?" she said at last.

"That is an interesting question." And yet another that I had never been asked before. I began to wonder just who this girl was. "From what I have gathered, the latent potential of the universe created me."

"What?" She sounded absolutely nonplussed, and I couldn't help but chuckle.

"I suppose that is a bit hard to understand." I glanced over my shoulder at her. "You have taken the more advanced science classes, correct?"

"Yeah."

"Good. Then you know the four fundamental forces of the universe?"

"Um, yeah." Her brow furrowed as she tried to recall them. "They're...gravitational, electromagnetic, strong nuclear, and weak nuclear, right?"

"Correct." I turned back to my drawing and added another long sweeping line. "Every significantly advanced species in the universe discovers those four forces. While they cannot generally be seen by the naked eye, these forces are still essentially physical. But there is another force that transcends these four, however. It exists much the same as I do, on a level beyond physical, and it governs all things. That force is potential."

"Potential? Like, possibility?" I heard her approach. She was interested now, both in what I was telling her, and in my creation.

"Exactly." She was next to me, her midnight hair just at the edge of my vision. "It is the driving force behind the cosmos themselves. It makes time flow, and everything that happens occurs because of it. The assassination of John F. Kennedy. The lunar riots in the D'zargo solar system. The interplanetary slave trade in the Grashialen Galaxy. The death of every star, and the birth of every planet. They actualize because at the time of their occurrence, the potential for their existence is greater than the potential for anything else."

"Okay, I think I get it. Kinda," she said, crossing her arms. "So, how did this potential make you?"

"I came into being when the very first death happened. A single cell, and at the moment of its demise the need for my existence was greater than anything else. So I became."

I still remembered that moment. My birth into glorious consciousness, when all existence was new, and every experience a wonder. There was no suffering then. No pain.

Grace leaned against the white board, coming into full view. She brushed a strand of hair back over her ear as she watched me work.

"So, you just suddenly showed up?" She snapped her fingers, "Just like that?"

"I like to think that there was a bit more circumstance to the occasion," I said. Grace laughed, and a warmth spread through me. "But, to put it simply, yes."

"Wow. I bet that was really something to see." It was a friendly little jab, and once again I stopped dead. I turned to her and found her smirking at me. She was relaxed, her body language speaking openness and camaraderie. Our eyes met, and it touched me more than I could say.

In all my eons of existence, I have been met with many emotions. Fear, anger, hatred, sadness. The greatest and strongest men and women have groveled before me. Few would stand in my presence, and fewer still would meet my gaze. I have met royalty and heroes and pioneers of industry that drove their people forward, but they were never the ones who treated me as something other than a source of fear. It was only souls like Grace, the normal and overlooked, that ever spoke with me. I thought it a blessing every time.

"It was something, indeed. The cell even cried. Of course, that might have had more to do with *why* I was created, rather than the actual happening," I said, making her laugh again. The sound spread throughout the room, pushing back the lingering shadows and making it bright and warm. For a moment, the emptiness I felt inside didn't seem so bleak, or so vast.

So I decided to take a chance.

"I once searched for God," I said it lightly, but those words were the hardest I had ever said.

"You did?" she said, excited.

"I did." Dots now, sweeping and systematic, bringing the lines to life. "Many Millennia ago. Before your Earth had even formed, I came to a soul from the Svehalkes people. One of the first civilizations in the universe. They were also the first to have organized religion. When I appeared before her, she dropped to her knees and beseeched Thanred, their God of Creation, to save her from my touch. She believed me to be Dagasta, their God of Evil, come to devour her immortal soul."

I worked faster as I spoke. Now lines, now shading and detail. A distraction from the fear of what I was telling this girl.

"It shook me to my very core. She was the high priestess of their temple, and I had never heard of, nor imagined anything like a God. It was harder to guide her on than any other soul since. But I was excited by these deities she spoke so emphatically of. Because they sounded so very much like myself."

My hands were almost a blur now.

"Eventually, other religions began to sprout across the universe as other civilizations developed. Their Gods were many and varied, and there was much disagreement among those that could interact, but at their heart they were more similar than not. I was fascinated, and hopeful, and finally my curiosity got the better of me. For nearly ten thousand Earth years, I abandoned my duties and searched the cosmos for these Gods."

"You didn't find anything, did you?"

She sighed when I shook my head.

"As I have said, I found no Gods. But that does not mean I found nothing."

Her head shot up.

"What did you find?" she asked, breathless.

"I discovered the beauty of existence," I said, heartened by her excitement. "From the moment of my creation, I was tethered to the duty that made me. Once free of it, I was able to see how beautiful this universe is."

Visions of what I beheld swam before my eyes, and my hand stilled.

"I have seen things that not even the greatest creative minds of your planet could dream of. I watched the birth of stars, and I witnessed their demise. And then, I fell in love."

She blinked. "With who?"

"With all of you," I said, and a smile stretched across my face. "With life and all its many vessels. I was able to watch it happen, not just guide its end. And it was glorious. I have marveled at the beauty of it since. Because no matter where I find it, or what form it takes, all life happens in the same way. You love, hate, fight, give, sacrifice, and push the boundaries of your own mortality in almost exactly the same way. And that discovery was beautiful."

We fell quiet then as Grace pondered my words. I continued my work, enjoying the companionable silence. My work took up half the board now. I stole a glance at her now and then. She leaned against the board still, arms crossed, a small smile playing about her lips. And there was wonder in her eyes.

"Perhaps I do have gifts to give," I whispered.

"What?" she said, looking up. I shook my head.

"Nothing." I added the last bit of shading and stepped back. "Finished."

Grace pushed off the board and came to stand next to me, taking it in. I waited patiently for her opinion. At last, she said, "It looks like a galaxy."

"It's the Nivdraxa Galaxy," I said, tracing the sweeping arms of it with my eyes.

"It's beautiful."

"It is," I said. One of the largest collections of stars and planets in the universe rotating in nine arms. I had done my best to portray that density, accentuating the largest stars, and the deep, dark, black hole that rested at its center. It truly was a magnificent sight.

"So, why did you draw it?" she said. I couldn't help but laugh.

"Because, it was there"—I stepped to the board and pointed to a location near the tip of one of the galaxy's arms—"on the planet Etgael-na in the Galino Solar system that the latent potential of the universe was first theorized, then discovered, qualified, and quantified."

"They actually found it? How?"

"Let me show you," I said. My power rose, and I pushed it into the drawing. Inch by inch I teased it from the board, manifesting the image until it existed in stark reality in the classroom. A perfect replica of the actual Galaxy. Grace watched in unbridled awe. The replica threw its light across her, making her shine like an angel.

I touched a spinning arm as it came by, and the galaxy magnified. The memories of stars, comets, and astral dust zoomed past us until a planet came into view, not unlike the one we were on now. Etgaelna as it appeared nearly fifty thousand Earth years before.

"It began with the mystics. Every civilization has them. Believers in the old ways, and the old superstitions." We zoomed in farther still to see the many men and women that belonged to Etgaelna's mystical orders.

"They're human," Grace cried out in astonishment.

"They are. The 'magic' they practiced was considered by most the stuff of fantasy. That is until one woman, a scientist, found that it was very much real. She believed that their magic was in fact an undiscovered universal force. She was correct, and her findings shook the world. She labeled this force 'Latent Universal Potential.'"

"Wait." Grace stepped in front of me. "Are you telling me that magic is real?"

"In essence, yes."

"Holy crap." She turned away, hair glittering in the planetary light.

"The 'magic' performed by the Etgaelnean mystics was not very impressive." Images of the robed men and women of the Temple of the Sisters danced before us. "Even the greatest of them could only ever harness the most minuscule amount of potential. The scientists believed they could do more, however."

Simahla stretched before us, an unfinished Sotiras at its center.

"As they studied the nature of this universal potential, they found that when combined with their will, they could literally perform miracles. So, they built a machine to gather, then manifest it. The called it the Sotiras, and its purpose was to cast the Great Working and end death."

We watched the people of Etgaelna traveled from all corners to be part of the great working. Scientists, and field workers. Young. Old.

Rich. Poor. All came and gave their will to the machine in hopes of escaping death. Then my heart leaped when Kholo made his mad rush to the Sotiras. Grace moved close, face inches away as she watched him run.

"Immortality?" she breathed. She turned from the images to me. "Did it work?"

"I was aware of their intentions by then, and I watched the machine complete its processes and set its purpose in motion." The hordes around the Sotiras were legion. Faces full of longing, excitement, and even fear as they waited to see if all the promises would be kept. "The Great Working was cast, and the people of Etgaelna vanished."

In the next second the hordes around the machine were gone. No pomp or circumstance. No great flash of light. Just there one second and gone the next. I prodded the manifestation with my power, and it shrank to show the entire planet, now completely bare of all life. Grace's eyes darted across the barren landscapes, confused.

"They just vanished?" she said, looking at me. I nodded. "Where did they go?"

"I wish I knew," I said sadly.

"Do you think that something went wrong?" she circled the now dead world.

"I have theories, but nothing more, and all knowledge of the undertaking disappeared with them." I waved my hand, and the dead planet and its galaxy disappeared. Grace blinked at the sudden gloom. "I never guided any of their souls over, and I have not encountered any of the life from Etgaelna elsewhere in the Universe. It is as if they ceased to be."

"I hope not." Grace slid into a desk. She stared at her hands, playing with the ring on her index finger. "It's too sad for them to just be gone. Maybe it worked, and they were taken somewhere with no death."

"I hope so. I truly do," I said, thinking of Kholo. I watched her play with her ring a moment before I decided to take another chance. I had come this far, trusted her this much, so why not? "I have never told anyone else this, but after pondering the disappearance of the Etgaelneans, I have a theory as to the identity of God. Would you like to hear it?"

She stilled and placed her hands on the desk in front of her. Her chair creaked as she sat back and said, "I would."

I took a breath. Let it out. "I believe you are God."

"Me?"

"You and every other mortal life," I said. "I believe that together, you are God."

Grace was quiet a moment, thinking. Then she said, "How?"

"God, by definition, is the most powerful being in creation. I have traversed this entire universe and seen the wonders you mortals achieve when united. Together, you perform miracles. After watching you do this time and again for eons, I have concluded that mortal life is the most powerful thing in existence. To my mind, the Etgaelneans confirmed it. You are, each and every one of you, a fragment of the divine." I pointed to her heart, which was far bigger than anyone deserved. "God is within you, not without."

A strange look crossed her face.

"We are God?"

"That is what I believe."

Her eyes fell to her desk, and once again silence reigned over us. A *knowing* beckoned. I ignored it. Not yet.

"I like that." She looked up and gave me a smile full of hope. The *knowing* nudged again, and I frowned. *Just a little more time. Please.*

"Thank you for sharing this with me. I know it was hard for you."

I furrowed my brow. "What makes you say that?"

"I'm not sure." She said, tilting her head to the side. "I just...*know*."

Her words shook me to the core. I opened my mouth to ask a thousand questions, and the *knowing* grasped my mind once more. Her time had come. So I asked her just one.

"Who are you, Grace Angelina Garcia?"

"I'm—" she bit her lip, looking for the right word. She nodded to herself and said, "A friend. I think."

"Yes. I think so too," I said with a little smile. The *knowing* hit me again, and my smile fled. "It seems our time together is at an end."

"What?" Grace said. I stood, and her eyes followed me up. I turned, reaching out to her as I did. She looked at my outstretched hand and her face fell. "Oh. Yeah."

"I am sorry." I say that to every soul, but I had never meant it more.

"It's okay," she said, her voice even and strong. "I think I'm okay."

"Take my hand."

She did, and I helped her to her feet. Then she threw her arms around me and hugged me once again. I hesitated for just a moment, then I put my arms around her as well.

And I hugged my friend.

We embraced for a long moment, then she stepped back looking embarrassed. She crossed her arms, shoulders hunched, suddenly nervous.

"So how does this work?" she asked.

"Come with me to the door." I beckoned for her to follow, and we made our way to the classroom's door. It was a gaudy thing. Crandall had covered it in silly images and clever sayings, all pertaining to Psychology. It was ugly, and the colors clashed horribly, but the sight made me happy. I peered through the window into the hall. A few students milled around outside, waiting for the classroom to be unlocked. I watched them for a moment, then I turned to Grace.

"Are you ready?"

Arms still crossed; she shook her head.

"No."

"No one ever is." I peeled apart reality once more. I sorted the threads and gathered those that made the door. Then I reached deep within my own strands, and from them I pulled a single thread, black as darkest night. I wove it into the others, and I let reality coalesce.

Then I opened the door.

The hallway was gone, leaving only darkness. Solid, and absolute. Grace gazed into the black, eyes wide, and reached out. Just before she touched the shadows, she blinked and jerked her hand back. Rubbing her hand, she said, "It's cold. Is that the other side?"

"No, it is the veil between." I gazed into the darkness. "All you have to do now is step through."

"That's it?"

"That's it." I stepped to Grace and placed a hand on her shoulder. She glanced at me and gifted me the barest ghost of a smile.

"Thank you for answering my questions," she said, staring down the darkness.

"Thank you for asking them."

"Can I ask one more?"

"You may."

"What's the other side like?"

I knew this question would come. It always does. So I gave her the words that Malik had given me.

"It might not be what you expected, but it will be far better than you feared."

She chuckled a little when she recognized the words, though her anxiety persisted. Looking up at me, she held out her hand.

"Ukufa, He Who Holds Your Hand in Shadow," she said, looking into my eyes. "Will you hold mine?"

Without hesitation, I reached out and took her hand.

"Always," I said, squeezing it. She squeezed back, then looked back to the door. She took a shuddering breath and stepped forward into the dark. It swallowed her, and her fingers slipped from mine at the last moment. Then she was gone.

"Goodbye, Grace Angelina Garcia." Alone now, I closed the door and held the handle tight. One single tear rolled down my cheek. The only one I would allow. I whispered, "Goodbye, my friend."

I let the handle go and stepped back just in time for the door to swing open. Crandall bustled in, followed by his students. I watched them take to their desks, their lives continuing as another part of mine withered and died. Crandall worked at his desk, occasionally responding to a student. The kids formed their groups. Some joked among themselves. Others finished homework. Still others spoke of Grace in hushed tones. I watched it all, and I grasped onto the light of the life I saw around me. I took strength from it, and I gathered myself together as best I could.

The wound of Grace's passing was much greater than I expected. But I didn't care. It felt good to feel close to her. To feel close to what I loved most. Life. Because I was tired, and it was getting harder to go on. Had been for a long time. Every soul I guided, every life I watched end, made the hole inside just a little wider. That emptiness was becoming too vast to stitch together again, and I knew the day would come that I would break once and for all.

When the last light winked out, and I closed the door on the death of the last of life, I wondered if I would cease to be then as well. Perhaps the darkness inside me would swallow me whole. Or perhaps I too would die, and another would open the door for me. I took in the vibrant life of Grace's classroom, and I sincerely hoped it would be the latter.

For then I too might learn what lies beyond.

About the author

Alexander G. R. Gideon's writing style can best be described by the phrase "and many people died". He's a multi-genre author of Historical Fantasy, Dark Fantasy, Sci-fi, and Horror. As the world's only Pan Librarian Wizard, he's an expert on most things, from High Magick and spirit summoning, to eldritch texts, to looking like the Kings, Queens, and other Monarchs you know you are! As an optician, he's a master at crafting light bending wearable artifacts! No matter what you wish, Gideon has a spell, book, or word for you!

Made in the USA
Columbia, SC
10 August 2024

39784950R00107